'You don't owe me

No, she didn't owe h ... invited him to stay?

A dark flame flickered in Clint's eyes. 'Do you think it would be wise?' he asked softly. 'The two of us alone in this house?'

The air was suddenly charged. Her heart began to throb and her throat went dry. She couldn't tear her gaze away from his eyes. 'I don't know,' she said. 'Would it be?'

Dear Reader

There's nothing more wonderful than celebrating the end of winter, with an exciting collection of books to choose from! Mills & Boon will transport you to all corners of the world, including two enchanting Euromance destinations—sun-drenched, exotic Madeira contrasting with scenic evergreen Wales. Let the spring sunshine brighten up your day by reading our romances which are bursting with love and laughter! So why not treat yourself to many hours of happy reading?

The Editor

Ever since **Karen van der Zee** was a child growing up in Holland she wanted to do two things: write books and travel. She's been very lucky. Her American husband's work as a development economist has taken them to many exotic locations. They were married in Kenya, had their first daughter in Ghana and their second in the United States. They spent two fascinating years in Indonesia. Since then they've added a son to the family as well. They now live in Virginia, but not permanently!

Recent titles by the same author:

PASSIONATE ADVENTURE
MAKING MAGIC

A LOVE UNTAMED

BY

KAREN VAN DER ZEE

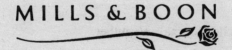

MILLS & BOON

MILLS & BOON LIMITED
ETON HOUSE, 18-24 PARADISE ROAD
RICHMOND, SURREY TW9 1SR

For Raja Kumis
King of the Moustaches

*First published in Great Britain 1994
by Mills & Boon Limited*

© *Karen van der Zee 1994*

*Australian copyright 1994
Philippine copyright 1994
This edition 1994*

ISBN 0 263 78420 7

*Set in Times Roman 10½ on 12 pt.
01-9403-50834 C*

Made and printed in Great Britain

CHAPTER ONE

IN THE silent night Livia heard the low rumble of a car approaching on the country road. There wasn't much traffic around here, so a car was something you noticed, especially at eleven at night. A cool spring breeze sweet with the scent of lilacs blew in through the open living-room window. She closed it and drew the old-fashioned curtains.

Dressed in a white cotton nightgown, she wandered through the quiet house, examining, for the umpteenth time, the contents—the old furniture, the antique clock, the dusty knick-knacks on the shelves—wondering if she had made a mistake coming here to spend the night by herself. The house seemed filled with ghosts, strange noises and musty smells. More so now that darkness had fallen over the empty countryside.

Well, it was not empty, really. There were cows and sheep and horses and probably rabbits, and frogs in the pond of course, and maybe spirits roaming the fields. But there were no houses containing living primates of the human variety for miles around. However, there would be one or more in the car coming down the road, she reminded herself. She wasn't sure if this was a reassuring thought or not.

The old house stood alone on a hill with a view of the Blue Ridge Mountains, and it was hers. Livia grinned at herself, feeling a sense of great excitement. It was a beauty, this old colonial country house, albeit that it was slightly ramshackle and needed a lot of work. But once she was done with it ... She could feel her hands itch for hammer and saw and paintbrush.

Ever since the closing this morning she'd been sorting and packing books and small items to go to the country auction-house. She'd felt distinctly indiscreet looking through drawers and cabinets and closets, examining all the private things that had once belonged to someone else, an old woman who had recently died and whom she had never known. She had bought the house with all its contents, because there had been no relatives to claim them and she had fallen in love with some of the furniture, some lovely old things, possibly antiques. But most of it was not of much value, just the ordinary slightly worn and shabby furniture of someone who had lived in the same place all her life, someone who'd grown comfortable with her own things and saw no need for replacement when upholstery grew thin or styles changed.

This morning she'd put her sleeping-bag, pillow and overnight bag in one of the upstairs's bedrooms. She unrolled the sleeping-bag and put it on top of the old quilted bedspread of one of the beds. Tomorrow morning Jack would be here and they'd go over the renovation plans and start clearing out the rooms. She couldn't wait to get started and her whole body was keyed up, as it always was when she started a new project. Once the rooms were empty, they'd start breaking down walls. She loved breaking down walls, creating light and space.

She heard the car coming closer. Pushing aside the faded flowered curtains, Livia looked out into the night, seeing the headlights approaching on the

curving road, illuminating the tall evergreens and the
blooming dogwoods, which looked white and lovely
as brides. The car was going very fast, or maybe it
just looked that way, and then it began to slow down.

It slowed down until it was barely going at all, and
then it turned into the long, curving driveway that
climbed up to the house.

Her heart slammed against her ribs. No one knew
she was here. Why would anyone come here so late
at night? It was almost eleven and no decent person
would call on someone else at this time uninvited.

Maybe this was not a decent person. The world was
full of people with evil intentions. All you had to do
was read the papers and turn on the television.

Oh, stop it, she said to herself. Maybe there was a
perfectly simple, innocent reason for someone to come
to the house. There had to be. She was basically a
cheerful person, and believing in happiness, joy and
love was so much more satisfying than being forever
worried about evil and disaster. Maybe the driver was
lost and had seen the lights, the only lights for quite
a distance. This was rural Virginia, hours and hours
away from Washington DC, where the day was not
complete without a murder and a couple of other as-
sorted crimes.

Nothing ever happened here. So she was told by
the plump and pleasant woman estate agent who'd
been born and bred in these parts and who knew every
living soul within a ten-mile radius. So she had said.

She heard the car door slam shut. Frozen to the
floor, she waited for the doorbell to ring. It did not.
Instead, she heard the heavy front door creak open,
then close again. It had been locked. She'd done it
with her own hands ten minutes ago. She should hide

in the wardrobe, climb out the window. Instead, she just stood there with her heart in her throat.

Heavy footsteps moved through the hall and living-room, the old wooden floors creaking ominously.

She was supposed to know what to do in situations like this. First: don't panic. Second: get away.

How? Jump out of a window?

Well, she'd not started taking karate lessons for nothing. She'd decided that if she was going to make a habit of making trips to exotic places around the world she needed to be proficient in some form of self-defence. You could never tell, could you? Maybe this was the time to test its usefulness in a real-life situation. If it failed, maybe she could get her money back. She choked back an hysterical giggle.

'Anybody home?' came a male voice. It was deep and gravelly and the sound vibrated in the air.

Her tongue lay paralysed in her mouth and she was too afraid to breathe. Well, almost. She found herself staring at her image in the dresser mirror. Boy, were her eyes big and dark! Her face looked white as the clichéd sheet in contrast to her black hair. Normally her skin was a warm Mediterranean tan, winter and summer, thanks to her Latin genes.

And then heavy steps came pounding up the stairs and there he was, standing right in front of her—the very devil indeed.

CHAPTER TWO

WILD black hair, penetrating black eyes, a bushy black beard. He was huge, looming over her, filling the small room with his bulk and the sense of dire threat. The very air shivered with it. As did her body. He wore faded jeans, disreputable running shoes and a wrinkled denim shirt with the sleeves rolled up, revealing brown, muscled arms. All of him was big and strong, emanating a primitive masculine power and virility.

However, she saw no horns, no fangs or whatever else devils were supposed to have. Neither did she see a gun or knife. He stared down at her with his black devil eyes.

This was not a comfortable moment. Standing there barefoot wearing nothing but a long white nightgown, her hair loose, she was not an image radiating power and control, she was quite sure. She must look like a terrified heroine in a Gothic novel. Petrified, she continued to stare at him. It did not bear considering what he might be contemplating as his dark eyes moved over her from top to bottom.

'Who are you?' he asked.

It was the tone of his voice that got her lungs going again. There was no threat or lechery in that deep voice, merely astonishment. This was extremely reassuring. Astonishment she could deal with. Astonishment was good.

She swallowed, then straightened her back, stretching as far as her meagre five feet four would allow, and put her hands on her hips.

'Who the hell are *you*?' she demanded.

His bushy brows shot up. 'I believe I asked the question first, angel.'

Angel. And that from the devil. Oh, God.

Her legs began to shake. 'I own this house and I want you out.' Her heart was racing but her voice was steady, which was nothing short of a miracle. However, he seemed not impressed.

His brows rose up even further. 'You own this house? I don't know where you get that idea. The house is mine.' He reached into his pocket and fished out a key. 'See? This is my key. It fits very nicely into the lock in the door of my house.' The hand dangling the key in front of her was big and brown and very strong. The other one was a perfect match. Hands that had seen hard physical labour. Her stomach churned.

'You may have a key, but I have a deed. The closing was this afternoon. The house is mine—all legal and above board. I signed all sorts of documents and the lawyers signed all sorts of documents and I wrote big cheques and then we all shook hands and smiled a lot. That's how it's done when you buy a house.' Oh, shut up! she said to herself. She always talked too much, but when she was nervous she positively gushed.

'You must have the wrong house.'

'That's crazy! Of course I don't have the wrong house! I bought *this* one.'

He frowned, then shrugged, raking a hand through his unruly hair. 'I'm not going to stand here and pursue a pointless argument with a woman in her nightgown. I'll find a way to disabuse you of your illusions tomorrow. What I need now is sleep.'

His arrogance infuriated her and she clenched her teeth hard. However, one thing she was noticing: in spite of his disreputable appearance, he spoke in complete sentences and his English sounded educated. Was this reassuring? Did it mean anything? Probably not a thing.

She willed her legs to stop trembling. 'You're not sleeping here,' she said with a conviction she didn't feel. 'Find yourself a hotel. There's a country inn five miles down the road. It's a lovely place, all white with red shutters, and the rooms have four-poster beds in them and you'll be perfectly comfortable there and...' She stopped herself. Here she was doing it again.

He rubbed his beard. 'It appears to me that you don't understand,' he said patiently, as if he were talking to a dimwitted child. 'Let me be more clear: I'm not going anywhere. This is *my* house, so *you* should leave and find yourself a room in the inn. However, I don't turn women in their nightgowns out into the street at this hour, so be my guest and stay the night.'

The audacity of the man! 'I'll call the police,' she said between clenched teeth.

An amused little grin curved his mouth. He stroked his beard thoughtfully. 'Oh, yes, good old Chuckie,' he said lazily. 'Sure, go ahead. And while you've got him on the line, tell him I won the bet and he owes me a hundred bucks.'

Her heart sank. There went that idea. Maybe he and Chuckie the sheriff were partners in crime. These things happened. You heard about it on TV: the nation's finest seduced by the rewards of crime. It was a disgrace. Calling Chuckie would obviously do no good. Now what? She couldn't think of a thing.

The man turned around. 'I'm going to sleep. Goodnight, angel.' And with that he strode out of the room. She didn't hear him go down the stairs, and when all became quiet and her legs were more steady, she gathered enough courage to find out where he'd parked himself.

She discovered him in one of the other bedrooms. He lay sprawled on top of the big double bed, fully clothed and out cold. He had taken off his Nikes and socks, and that was about it. Like the rest of him, his feet looked big.

It was easy to see that neither flood, hurricane nor earthquake was going to move this man. He was dead to the world and by the looks of it he was going to stay that way for a while. Which meant she was going to be safe for a while.

She looked at the comatose shape and felt a shiver go down her spine. Where had he come from? Maybe he'd been driving for a long time. Maybe he had escaped from prison, stolen a car... Maybe she should have a look at the car, check out the licence plates.

She tiptoed down the stairs, although there was no need to be so quiet. Her footsteps weren't going to wake him out of his stupor. In the hall by the front door she saw a huge duffel bag with airline tags. United Airlines. He'd arrived at Washington Dulles, but he could have come from anywhere. The name tag was a coded American Express affair that would only reveal its secrets to a computer. Then she noticed the papers sticking out of a side-pocket. Ticket carbons? It would supply the passenger's name and flight information. She hesitated.

Why had the gods burdened her with an oversupply of principles? She didn't snoop in other people's drawers and she didn't peep into their bathroom medicine cabinets. She didn't cheat on her taxes. She didn't steal ashtrays from hotel rooms; she didn't even take the little soaps and bottles of shampoo. And she never lied. Well, almost never.

She did not go through other people's papers, either.

She stared at the corner of grey peeping out from the duffel-bag pocket.

Well, she had the right, didn't she? Shouldn't she know the identity of a stranger who'd forced himself into her house and refused to leave? A dangerous-looking stranger now asleep under her roof?

Of course she did.

She went down on her knees, took the oblong booklet out of the pocket and leafed through the flimsy carbons, peering hard at the faint lettering to decipher it. Clint Bracamonte, it said. It seemed to fit him. He certainly didn't look like a Jimmy Johnson.

It took a few minutes to piece together his itinerary from the collection of ticket carbons, but then she had it and it made her heart beat faster—not with fear this time, but from pure excitement.

Balikpapan-Jakarta-Hong Kong-San Francisco-Washington DC.

Balikpapan! Balikpapan was a town in the Indonesian province of Kalimantan on the island of Borneo, a wild place full of jungle and rough rivers and tiny villages and tribal people living traditional lives. She knew her geography, which was not so surprising since she had lived in many places in the world due to a globetrotting father who was a career diplomat. They'd resided in Jakarta, Indonesia, in Kuala Lumpur, Malaysia, in Dar es Salaam, Tanzania, in Geneva, Switzerland, and other places of which she had no memory because she'd been too young.

She put the papers back in the duffel-bag pocket and straightened. She opened the heavy door. The hinges squealed in agony and she winced at the sound. The perfumy fragrance of lilacs greeted her. She stepped on to the front porch and the old wood creaked under her feet. Everything was making noise, setting her nerves on edge. She took a look at the car. As expected, it was a rental he'd procured at the airport, a silver-grey Ford Taurus.

She shivered in the cold night air and went back into the house, tiptoed up to her own bedroom and sat on the side of the bed. Jack would come early tomorrow morning. For now she should just go to bed. Mr Bracamonte had flown straight from Balikpapan to Washington without a stopover—two days without sleep, across the international date line and many time zones, his body clock gone haywire. He wasn't going to wake up for a while.

Why did he think the house was his? It was crazy, impossible. She couldn't think. She was simply too tired. A long afternoon of hard physical labour topped off with a big dose of heart-stopping terror tended to be exhausting.

She crawled into the sleeping-bag and closed her eyes. She should have lain awake anxious and afraid, but, strange as it might seem, she didn't. She drifted right off and slept like a baby.

* * *

She awoke with the birds, which sang euphorically in the trees. She'd left the window open and the April morning was glorious, the air crisp like chilled champagne. For a moment she luxuriated in a sense of wellbeing—a very short moment, because her mind suddenly produced the image of the dark stranger who'd found his way into the house late last night. Black eyes, black hair, black beard.

Oh, God. She closed her eyes. Well, she was alive and well and she hadn't even had to employ her meagre karate skills.

She locked the bathroom door and had a quick shower, then dressed in jeans and a bright red cotton sweater. Red was good. It made a statement. It showed confidence and power. She had a hunch she'd need some once Clint Bracamonte was awake. Hopefully that wouldn't be until Jack had arrived.

She put on socks and trainers and tied her hair back in a ponytail and made up her face. It was no genetic accident that she had straight black hair and brown eyes. She was American by upbringing and citizenship, but her ancestral background sported Greeks, Italians, Hungarians, and even an outcast gypsy woman who'd had the audacity to fall in love with a gorgio. Her mother had researched the family tree with true passion, travelling to Europe to find out as much as she could, discovering long-lost relatives—a dentist, a goatherd, a butcher, a housewife, and, lo and behold, a toothless Greek great-great-grandma of one hundred and seven wearing black, totally lucid and not about to depart. She drank two shots of ouzo every day.

The family tree revealed many things. It was not so strange that her dearest passion was travel: gypsy genes. Also, she loved colourful clothes and dangling earrings, and she'd discovered a taste for ouzo. Her friends insisted it had to be genetic, because how else was it possible to like that vile stuff?

Quietly she slipped down the stairs into the kitchen, only to find that she had miscalculated. The man was standing by the sink, filling the kettle. The same huge male that had walked into her house last night—black eyes, black hair, but minus the bushy black beard. Her heart turned over. He looked fantastic. She couldn't help thinking it. It was the truth. The evil had gone out of his appearance and what was left was a lot of very disturbing male sex appeal. He plunked the kettle on the stove and turned on the burner.

'Well, good morning,' he said, noticing her stand by the door.

'Good morning,' she returned, feeling the very air around her quiver with sudden tension.

He wore clean clothes—cotton trousers and a blue T-shirt. His hair was damp from the shower, still too long but tamed by the water, at least temporarily. His eyes were still the same penetrating black and the part of his face where yesterday had flourished the bushy beard now revealed a strong, square jaw. His face was all hard angles, his features well-defined. Energy radiated from him.

His gaze swept over her, then back up to her face. 'Are you the same woman I met last night, the one wearing that long, lacy nightgown? Or was that merely a lovely vision in my dreams?'

Her stomach tightened and her pulse leaped. 'That was me,' she said, not being able to think of anything more brilliant or profound. It was a pretty nightgown, true, but she wished she'd been wearing functional unisex pyjamas instead. Only she didn't own any. She liked beautiful lingerie—possibly because it felt good to put on something soft and feminine after spending a long, hard day in old jeans and a T-shirt covered with dust and paint and wallpaper paste.

He took two mugs out of one of the cabinets. 'Coffee?' he asked politely.

'Thank you, yes,' she answered, equally politely. Well, that was the way she'd been brought up. It sort of came out automatically, but she realised the absurdity of the whole situation as soon as she heard her own courteous reply. The man had invaded her house and now he was playing host.

The groceries she'd bought yesterday had been taken out of the paper bags and spread out on the table. Instant coffee, chocolate bars, bread, peanut butter, thick orange marmalade, strong French mustard. He'd obviously taken charge and acted as if he had every right to be here in this kitchen.

He opened one of the cabinets, took out two plates and put them on the table, then opened a drawer and found knives and forks. It did not escape her that he didn't search for these items. He knew exactly where they were. It was not a good sign. A tiny flame of apprehension began to flicker in her mind. She suppressed it. Maybe he'd checked things out earlier.

'Make yourself at home,' she said coolly.

'I am at home,' he returned. 'So tell me, what is your name?'

'What is yours?'

'May I point out to you that a question requires an answer, not another question?'

'You may point all you want. What's your name?'

His mouth curved in faint mockery. 'Clint
Bracamonte. What's yours?'

'Olivia Jordan.'

'Olivia.' He spoke her name as if tasting it, narrowing his eyes, considering. 'Nice name. I like that.
Now, Olivia, is this all there is for food? What were
you planning to eat for breakfast? Peanut butter
sandwiches?'

'Something wrong with that?' In Kalimantan people
probably ate rice for breakfast, as they did in much
of the Far East.

'Nothing at all,' he said calmly. 'I was only asking.'

She opened the freezer compartment of the refrigerator and extracted a couple of frozen breakfast
burritos in paper wrappings. 'Actually, I was going
to have one of these.' She put them on the counter
and turned on the small toaster oven.

'Breakfast burritos?' He examined the frozen food,
reading the information printed on the wrapper.
'Good God, what are they going to come up with
next?'

'They're good,' she said. 'Eggs, cheese, ham, the
works. All the protein you need.' And all the choles-
terol you didn't. 'And they're real easy. All you do is
heat them up in the oven. Haven't you ever seen these
before? Where have you been?' She couldn't help
herself.

'Not anywhere in the so-called civilised world,' he
said promptly.

So she had discovered from his ticket carbons, but
of course he didn't know that, and she wasn't about
to admit that she'd been snooping through his papers.

'And where was that?' she asked casually.

'Nowhere you'd know.'

That's what you think, she told him silently, annoyed with his arrogance. She looked at him squarely. 'Try me.'

Obviously he didn't deem this a worthy challenge, because he simply ignored it. Instead he poured boiling water into the mugs and handed her one.

Well, how many people in rural Virginia had ever heard of Balikpapan? Not too many. Yet his condescending attitude was definitely insulting. Mr High and Mighty, Mr Globetrotter with an attitude problem.

'You're giving me the evil eye,' he said with a sardonic twist of his lips.

'It's my gypsy blood,' she said lightly, and took a drink from her coffee.

'Ah,' he said slowly. 'Gypsy blood. Very intriguing. Is that what gives you the fire in your eyes?' He flicked a finger at her ponytail. 'And that gorgeous dark hair?'

Instinctively, she took a step back. It had been a casual gesture, the way he had touched her hair, yet it had set off instant sparks of fire inside her. 'Watch it,' she said. 'I do spells, too.' She walked out the back door into the bright spring morning, taking her cup with her. His presence was dark and disturbing and made her long for light and cheer. He made her uneasy with those black, mysterious eyes and that big, muscled body, all male virility and power. She didn't want him in her house.

Yet it was not fear for her physical well-being that made her uncomfortable. She saw power, strength and energy, but no violence. There was something else that disturbed her, that made her heart beat faster, her senses sharpen. Something that set off strange vibrations and tremors.

The back porch was big and had a view of the grounds with its many blooming white and pink dogwoods, and numerous azaleas in a luxuriant riot of colour. It was a fairy-tale garden. She leaned on the wooden railing and watched the squirrels racing up and down the large oak trees just starting to bud into leaf. Everywhere birds chirped in exuberant harmony. Spring was springing and all was light and cheer.

She loved this place. She'd remodel it as a big family home, but it would be perfect as a bed-and-breakfast, a hideaway where stressed-out yuppie couples could come for rest, relaxation and romance.

She sighed. Romance. She wouldn't mind a little romance herself. Actually, she wanted a lot more than a little romance. She was twenty-eight and she wanted a man for the long haul, meaning that she wanted a lot of romance for a long time, preferably for the rest of her life, another fifty years or so. A half-century. Finding a man good enough to last you for a half-century wasn't an easy proposition.

The kitchen screen door squeaked and Clint appeared next to her, leaning brown muscled arms on the railing.

He was awfully close, or maybe it just seemed that way. Her body reacted instantly, tensing, as if her every cell was aware of his presence. She smelled soap. She stared straight ahead at the oak tree, fighting the impulse to move away. She didn't want him to know he disturbed her.

'We need to talk,' he said. 'My mind was not exactly crystal-clear last night, and it unfortunately did not retain the information about the reason for your presence in my house.'

Her hands clamped hard around her coffee-cup. 'It's my house. I bought it, I paid for it, I own it, it's mine. Is that clear enough?'

He shook his head. 'Unfortunately, it's not clear at all. If *I* didn't sell it, *you* couldn't have bought it.'

'I've never met a man who owned a house furnished like this one unless he was an eighty-year-old widower.' Doilies on the backs of chairs. A collection of porcelain figurines, needlepoint cushions, ruffled curtains, cabbage-rose wallpaper. *Good Housekeeping* magazines twenty years old.

He observed her calmly. 'Then you've learned something today and it's only seven in the morning. Congratulations.'

She wanted to throw her coffee at him, but only barely controlled herself. 'The house belonged to an old lady. She died. I bought the house.'

'The old lady was my grandmother and she left the house to me. I have a will to prove it.'

For a moment she felt panic. Had she been the victim of some crooked scheme? It was true that she'd got the house for a good price, but not such a good price as to make it suspiciously low. In her mind's eye she saw the round, friendly face of the estate agent who had sold her the house. The lady who had told her that there was no crime in these parts, the lady who had shown her the picture of her baby granddaughter—a beautiful baby, not at all the sort of baby that would have a criminal for a grandmother.

She was not the victim of a crooked deal. She could not afford to believe it. If the sale had been a fraudulent one, she might lose everything. There'd be nothing left—no money, no trip to the Amazon jungle. In fact, she'd be in debt. It was enough to make you panic and break out in a sopping sweat. Only, she refused. She simply refused to panic.

All the papers had been in order. The whole process had been completely ordinary and routine and she was no dummy. This wasn't the first time she'd bought a house. In the past five years she'd bought, fixed up and sold five residences in all. This was the sixth. She knew what she was doing. She crossed her arms in front of her chest and gave him a stony stare.

'I suggest you check with your lawyer about that will,' she said, as coolly professionally as she could manage in the circumstances, 'and with Boswell and Armis in Charlottesville. They dealt with the estate.'

His mouth curved fractionally. 'Oh, I certainly will.' And you're not going to get away with anything, his tone implied. He took a swallow of his coffee and surveyed the view with obvious appreciation. He did not say anything, but she could tell from his face. A good face. Strong, determined, yet with a certain undefinable sensuality... Good lord, what was she thinking?

He turned to face her again. 'You said you bought the house. Anyone else involved in this little scheme? A husband perhaps?'

She glared at him. 'Nobody is involved in any kind of a scheme. And I don't have a husband.' Why had she said that? It was none of his business.

He was too close for comfort. She finished the last of her coffee and pushed herself away from the railing. In the kitchen she opened a carton of orange juice, filled two glasses and put them on the table.

This was not a good situation. What was she going to do with this man in her house? How was she going to get rid of him? Here she was, having breakfast with the intruder. It was completely absurd.

He came in and poured more water into the kettle and put it on the stove.

She fixed her gaze on his broad back. 'Mrs Coddlemore died two months ago. If she was your grandmother, why didn't you come here sooner to handle the estate?'

'I didn't know she had died until ten days ago.' He turned and sat down at the table.

'Why didn't you know until ten days ago? Didn't anyone notify you?'

'Yes, they notified me, but the news didn't reach me until ten days ago.'

'Where were you? The moon? Antarctica? The jungle?' She looked straight at his face.

'The jungle,' he said. 'Only these days we call it the rainforest.'

'Yes, I've heard. Which rainforest?'

'Kalimantan.'

She nodded. 'Borneo, the Indonesian part.'

His eyes narrowed and she felt a thrill of triumph. She smiled brightly. 'I have this thing for geography. Maps have always fascinated me, ever since I was little. All those exotic places! All those fascinating countries and mysterious islands!' She sighed. 'Well, let's eat.'

The breakfast burritos were heated through and ready to eat. She placed one on each plate and he picked up his knife and fork and cut into the tortilla-wrapped bundle. Melted cheese oozed out. Egg and ham came into view. He began to eat without comment.

'So, what do they eat for breakfast in Kalimantan?' she asked, having trouble with the silence between them. Silence made her nervous. She wanted it filled up with something—conversation.

He shrugged. 'Rice, wild boar, fish, whatever.' The water boiled and he pushed himself to his feet and made more coffee. The burrito finished, he ate two more slices of toast. Then he got up and marched to the kitchen door. He turned and met her eyes.

'I'll see you tonight.' It was more than a statement. It was a promise. He opened the door and strode out.

She ran to the phone as soon as she'd heard the car drive away. But the lawyer's offices weren't open for business yet, nor the estate agent. Well, she wasn't going to sit here and be paralysed. She was going to go on with the job.

The skip had been delivered the day before, and she began cheerfully tossing in junk and rubbish. She took down the old dusty window treatments and tossed them out, except the drapery linings which she could use as painting drop cloths. Soon the truck from Rommel's Auction Barn would come and haul off the first load of stuff she didn't want to keep—books and knick-knacks and much of the furniture.

Then the phone rang. It was Jack, her brother the architect, and the familiar sound of his voice was instantly comforting. However, not comforting was the news that his car had given up the ghost that very morning.

'Would it be a terrible tragedy if I didn't make it today?' he asked. 'I'll have it back by tonight and I'll come tomorrow.'

Livia felt her heart sink. She considered telling Jack what had transpired, then thought better of it. If she did, all four of her brothers would descend on the house to rescue her within hours. This was very nice, of course; it made her feel loved and cared for, but it might, in actual fact, not be helpful. First she wanted to make sure what the situation really was.

What the situation really was, the lawyer told her a while later when she called again, was that the old lady had made a new will only days before she had passed away. In that will it was stipulated that the house be put up for sale and the revenue deposited in the bank in the name of her grandson who was incommunicado in the Borneo jungle, but who would show up sooner or later. The lawyer himself had been appointed the executor of the estate and she had nothing to worry about. Nothing fishy going on.

'What's the name of the grandson?' she asked, holding her breath.

'Let me check,' said the lawyer. 'Oh, here it is. Clinton Bracamonte. Why do you want to know?'

'He just emerged from the jungle and he's trying to claim the house.'

From the dining-room window Livia noticed the silver-grey Ford come up the drive and instantly felt her heart start racing. The truck from Rommel's Auction Barn was sitting in the drive, full of a load of chairs and tables and boxes with dishes and plates and glasses, none of them of great value. She'd spent all day sorting through cabinets and drawers, deciding what to keep and what to sell. She was tired and dirty.

The dining-room was cleared and she was almost finished taking up the old carpeting.

Clint came out of the car, strode up to the truck, took one look at it, said something to the driver and turned abruptly. He marched up the front porch, opened the door and slammed it.

'Olivia!'

'I'm in the dining-room,' she called out. She went down on her knees and started rolling up the last strip of carpeting. Underneath the padding lay a beautiful oak floor. She'd leave the padding to protect the wood during the painting process.

The next moment Clint loomed in the door and stared. His dark eyes scanned the room and what he saw obviously did not please him. Of course, she had not expected him to be pleased. That was why her heart was hammering against her ribs. The air was electric.

He advanced into the room. 'What the hell have you been doing?' he asked, his voice low and furious.

'I'm clearing the place out,' she said as calmly as she could. 'It makes it a lot easier to do the renovation work.' The room looked bare. All the curtains gone, the walls empty of pictures, the furniture removed.

'These were my grandmother's things!'

'They are my things now,' she said, steeling herself. 'And I can do with them as I please. If you want them, buy them back from Rommel's Auction Barn. I'm sure Mr Rommel will make you a deal for the lot. He seems like a nice guy.'

There was a loaded silence. She felt a shiver crawl up her spine as she looked at his hard face, his penetrating black eyes.

'All right,' he said slowly, 'let's talk.'

CHAPTER THREE

LIVIA'S heart was pounding. He was not a man who suffered defiance, but she'd be damned if she'd let him intimidate her. 'There's nothing to talk about. This is my house and I want you out.' She went on rolling up the heavy, awkward carpeting. Dust motes floated in the sunlight streaking through the window.

Clint Bracamonte reached out, took her arms and pulled her to her feet. 'I said, let's talk,' he said quietly.

Her reaction was automatic. A couple of swift moves and she was free of his grip. 'Keep your hands off me,' she said coldly.

He laughed. 'That was very impressive, I have to admit.'

His reaction infuriated her. How dared he be amused? 'Next time you won't laugh. You'll hurt.'

He nodded solemnly, but a spark of humour glinted in his eyes. 'I'll keep that in mind. Karate *and* gypsy spells. You're a dangerous woman.'

She gave him a withering look which seemed to have no effect on him at all. Not that she really had any hope of affecting him; he didn't look like a man who'd feel threatened by anything, and certainly not by a lightweight female.

He pushed his hands into his pockets. 'Now, I have a proposition to make,' he said casually.

'I'm not interested in your propositions.'

'I made some enquiries,' he went on, unperturbed. 'And you're right, you bought the house, and it's yours.'

She inclined her head in mockery. 'Thank you,' she said, pseudo-polite. 'I understand you are the recipient of the money from the sale.'

'Correct. Unbeknownst to me, my grandmother had made a new will. Apparently she thought I'd rather have the money than be burdened with the house.'

'Good. Then it's all cleared up.'

'No, it's not. My grandmother thought wrong. I *do* want the house. So this is what we'll do. I'll buy the house back from you and give you a five-per-cent profit.'

She laughed. She simply couldn't help it. The audacity of the man was amazing. Did he think he could tell her what to do? Did he think that she would let this opportunity be taken from her just like that? She met his eyes unflinchingly. 'No, sir, this is *not* what we will do. I bought the house because I wanted it.'

'I'll give you a ten-per-cent profit,' he said calmly.

'No.'

His eyes narrowed. 'What do you want?'

'I want this house. It's a beautiful old house and I'm going to fix it up and make it even more wonderful. I'm going to make it a masterpiece of renovation,' she said loftily. 'Then I'll sell it for every penny it's worth to someone who'll recognise the value of it. That's the business I'm in. That's what I do for a living.' And she was very, very good at it. She had an eye for what would work, and what would not, and a brother who was an architect.

House renovation hadn't exactly been the career she'd dreamed of since she was five. She'd wanted to be a ballerina then. She'd fallen into the remodelling business by coincidence, helping out a friend of her mother's restore a trashed townhouse in Georgetown, a yuppie Washington DC neighbourhood. I can do this, too, she'd thought, and with a loan from her father she'd done just that. She'd made a huge profit. She'd paid off the loan and bought another house, repeating the process.

Now, six years later, she was making a respectable living, which was very nice because she loved to travel, which she did in between projects. She loved travelling even more than remodelling houses, which was a lot of fun. Having a job you loved doing was a great blessing, and she was well aware of it. She loved counting her blessings, which were many.

Clint was not happy with her reply. His jaw worked. 'I don't want it renovated,' he said tightly.

'That's too bad, because it's not for you to decide.' She couldn't help feeling a nasty little twinge of triumph. She crossed her arms in front of her chest. 'Besides, it's *stupid* not to fix this house up. Have you seen the electricial wiring? It's *ancient*! It's a *fire hazard*! And the plumbing is medieval.' She was beginning to like this man less and less. Which was not promising because she had liked him not at all to start with. He was arrogant and presumptuous and condescending.

He was also dangerously handsome and sexy.

All in all, a toxic mixture and not one that was easily dealt with. There was an innate sexuality about him that was hard to miss. It was nothing he did or said in particular. It was just *there*, an aura, something radiating from him, something that affected her more than she was willing to admit. It seemed so primal

that it frightened her a little. After all, she was not
the kind of woman who let herself be swept away just
by a good body and a handsome face. She wanted
more, a whole lot more.

He was observing her with an infuriating glint in
his eyes. 'There's more to you than meets the eye, is
there?'

'I wouldn't know,' she said coldly. 'I've never had
a first impression of myself.'

His mouth curved in amusement and for a moment,
a long, endless moment, their eyes were locked in a
wordless sizing up of each other, a recognition of each
other, an acknowledgement. Her body grew warm,
her pulse throbbed and knees began to tremble. It was
hard to breathe. It was terrifying. He hadn't even
touched her. She broke her gaze away. She wanted to
run away, out of that room with its dangerous vibrations, but she fought the impulse.

'If you'll excuse me, I have work to do.' She heard
the nervous quiver in her voice and prayed he wouldn't
notice.

Before she'd gone down on her knees again, he'd
bent down and without a word rolled up the last strip
of heavy carpeting and slung it over his shoulder as
if it were nothing more than a wet towel.

'In the skip?' he enquired.

'Yes.' She watched him go, thrown completely off
balance. She didn't like the feeling. One moment he
was insufferably autocratic, the next he made a helpful
gesture like this—helping her do the very thing he was
angry at her for doing. Through the window she saw
him toss the carpeting effortlessly into the skip. He
had dropped the subject of buying the house. He had
not insisted, or made threats. However, she was not

deluding herself in thinking the issue was dismissed and the discussion over. Clint Bracamonte was not a man who gave up.

He strode up to his car and opened the back, taking out two paper grocery bags. He put them down in the kitchen, then washed his hands before taking out the contents.

Strawberries, asparagus, sirloin steak, French bread, and double cream, butter, mushrooms, onions, the makings for a salad, and a small selection of French cheeses. A bottle of red wine with an impressive label joined the luscious foodstuffs on the counter.

'What do you think you're doing?' she asked.

He smiled at her, a true blue Boy Scout smile that threw her even more off-balance. 'I'm inviting you to dinner,' he said, 'to repay you for your hospitality.'

She was lost for words.

What could she possibly say? Get out of my house and take your steak and strawberries with you? She'd be nuts. She'd worked like a horse all day, surviving on a breakfast burrito, a peanut butter sandwich and a couple of chocolate bars. She was famished. She stared longingly at the food he'd taken out of the bag. Why eat chicken soup and crackers if she could dine on steak, asparagus and strawberries and cream? And wine, too.

He studied her face, waiting for an answer. 'So, what do you say? It looks to me as if you could use a good meal.' His voice was even. 'You put in quite a day's work.'

So she had. She straightened. 'I'd love a good meal.' It was the truth, and she wasn't in the habit of lying. Also, it was difficult to resist him. She had to admit it. Besides, there was no harm in a meal together, was there?

'Excellent.' He reached in a drawer, found a corkscrew and opened the bottle. 'How about a glass before dinner? Or are you a purist and want your wine to breathe first?'

'I'm a purist only when it's convenient. I'd like a glass now.'

Wine in hand, she left the kitchen, allowing him the freedom to do his cooking all by himself. She wasn't much of a cook herself. It simply wasn't one of her talents. However, she did like eating good food. Eating in nice restaurants worked very well, or at her mother's house. Her mother did like cooking. Only her mother, as well as her father, were not presently in the neighbourhood. The government had sent them to Stockholm, Sweden.

Livia went into the living-room and started emptying drawers and packing more boxes, sipping wine. A vague, uneasy feeling stirred inside her. She pushed it back. Nonsense. No reason to feel this way. No obligation, no duty. The house was hers. Everything in it was hers. She'd bought it fair and square with her own money.

Yet the little fairy inside her was not happy.

When she was little, her mother had explained about that little voice inside her that sometimes bothered her when she'd done something wrong. It belonged to her personal little fairy of virtue that lived in her heart. The fairy loved her very much. The fairy told her what was right and wrong. As a little girl she had imagined the little fairy with small fluttering wings of gossamer silk, and a tiny candle in her delicate little hands, a candle to guide her on the right path.

As she was packing the boxes, the fairy fluttered nervously. Livia told the fairy to go for a nice long walk. The fairy did not oblige. Livia kept on packing. Ashtrays, doilies, chipped vases, a stained tea cosy, a box of buttons, a worn-out Scrabble game, a soft baby toy. She smiled as she looked at the brightly coloured cloth ball. Someone must have left it here. She tossed it into the box.

Her hands were dry from all the dust and all the washing she'd been doing. This wasn't the sort of job that was compatible with soft hands and lovely, long nails, polished burnished copper or honey rose.

Clint called her less than an hour later. By then she was practically passing out from hunger. The table had been set. He'd even found a white tablecloth and candles. They were baby-blue and sat in crystal candlesticks. She liked the candlesticks. She was going to keep them for herself.

'My grandmother loved these candlesticks,' he said. 'She'd brought them with her from Poland when she and my grandfather emigrated. They were a wedding gift.'

Oh, great. Now she was going to have to feel guilty. No, she was already feeling guilty. Inside her the little fairy was practically screaming.

'You can have them,' she heard herself say. Guilt was a nasty emotion and not one she intended to cultivate.

'I'll buy them from you.'

Their eyes met. 'I can't have you buy back your own grandmother's favourite candlesticks,' she said. 'Just take them.'

'All that businesslike behaviour covers up a soft heart, doesn't it?' he said with a crooked smile.

'Oh, please, spare me,' she said derisively and concentrated on her food, which was delicious. She wanted to ask him who he was, what he was. But something inside her kept her from asking. The less she knew, the better it was. She already knew about a Polish grandmother and wedding-gift candlesticks. She wanted him out of her way. If he didn't like her carting out all the old furniture, what was he going to say when the contractor arrived and some of the walls were going to come down?

'What were you doing in the rainforest?' she heard herself ask. She couldn't help herself. She wanted to know. 'Catching tropical birds and smuggling them out? Cutting down the trees for tooth-pick companies?'

He raised his brows. 'Do you always think so well of people, or is it just me?'

She gave him a wide-eyed, innocent look. 'Just a few wild guesses, that's all.' She smiled. 'May I assume you're doing something more honourable?'

'I'm involved in a research project. I study the interaction between the indigenous people and their rainforest environment.'

'Ah, a scientist.'

'I'm an ecological anthropologist.'

It sounded very impressive. She *was* impressed. 'Do you live with the people you're studying?' she asked.

He nodded. 'I live in a traditional longhouse village.'

'*Live*? Are you going back?'

'Yes.' He was on home leave for two months, he said, working for the University of Virginia, giving lectures and interviews in various places. After that he would go back to Kalimantan. He gave her this information in short, crisp sentences.

'Why do you want this house, then? You're not going to live here anyway.'

He gave her a dark, inscrutable look. 'For starters, I intended to live here for the next couple of months while I'm in the country. And more importantly, this was my grandmother's house and the place I call home.'

The place I call home. Had he no family, then? No parents? The guilt stirred some more and again she forced it down. 'I see,' she said, cutting a piece of steak. 'Obviously your grandmother had other ideas.'

His jaw tightened and he did not respond. For a while they ate in tense silence.

'What are your plans for this house?' he asked then. His voice was coolly casual.

She swallowed a piece of steak. 'I told you. I'm going to renovate it, then sell it.'

'What sort of renovation do you have in mind?'

She didn't want to discuss it. Yet he was not being unreasonable asking these questions. Anyone coming to the house could conceivably be interested in what she intended to do. It was not exactly a terribly sensitive, private, personal thing. Only it was. She glanced at her plate.

'I'm going to add another bathroom upstairs and modernise the two existing ones and put in a whirlpool bath. The kitchen is going to be overhauled.' There was more. Walls were going to come down, a sunroom added. She didn't tell him.

'Are you an architect?'

'No. I'm good with hammer and saw and paint.'

He studied her face. 'There's a whole lot more to
it than that.'

So there was. 'I know what I'm doing. I've done
it plenty of times before.'

'Ah, a handywoman.' He poured more wine. She
kept looking at his hands, which aroused disturbing
images in her mind.

If she weren't feeling so off-balance, it would be
very pleasant, actually, sitting here in such a civilised
fashion eating a wonderful meal, fixed by a man. The
man she married would have to be willing and able
to cook. This was one of the prerequisites, if not the
most important one. Most important was, of course,
his eternal devotion.

He buttered a piece of bread. 'Are you going to
have contractors, plumbers, electricians, workmen
around here?'

'Yes. All the wiring is going to be replaced and most
of the plumbing.'

'And you're dealing with these men on your own?'

She raised a quizzical brow. 'Yes, I am.' And she
was very good, too. Growing up with four brothers
was good for many things. 'Is there a problem with
that?'

'I imagine there could be many. Many men are not
comfortable taking orders from women, especially not
if they perceive their manly domain invaded.'

She nodded. 'Men with shaky egos, yes, I've
noticed. You have to know how to handle them.'

His mouth quirked. 'And you do?'

'I'm an expert.'

Humour sparked in his eyes. 'No pushover,
are you?'

'I grew up with four brothers. I learned to hold my own.' Unfortunately she wasn't sure she'd be able to hold her own with this man.

His eyes narrowed, scrutinising her, assessing her, and she felt again that odd reaction—the warmth, that hypnotic feeling of not being in control. His black eyes seemed to look straight inside her very soul.

She didn't want anybody looking into her soul uninvited, and certainly not this man. She got up from the table. 'Thank you for a delicious dinner,' she said nicely. 'Now, if you'll excuse me, I'll have to go back to work.'

She hoped he would leave now. Put his things in his car and go. A while later she heard strange sounds coming from outside and looked out of the window. Clint was standing on a ladder, sawing a big dead limb off one of the old oaks. Transfixed, she watched the movement of his body, noticing the effortless control he had over it. Powerful arms, a strong back straining under his shirt. The sound of the limb crashing to the ground startled her out of her trance. She closed her eyes for a moment and took a deep breath.

She stayed out of his way for the rest of the evening, knowing he wasn't leaving, not knowing what to do about it. She slept restlessly, aware of his presence down the hall, seeing in her mind the intent look in his black eyes, feeling apprehension shiver through her body.

The next morning he was gone by the time she came downstairs, but when she looked in his room his things were still there. He hadn't given up.

Well, she hadn't expected him to, had she?

She was angry and relieved at the same time.

*　　*　　*

'I thought I'd come along and see if I could help,' said Sara. 'My mom's babysitting the kids.' Sara had short red hair, lots of freckles and a big smiling mouth. She was Jack's wife and Livia loved her. The two of them had arrived around ten that morning and Jack had brought the blueprints for the remodelling work.

Livia and Jack had had the opportunity to tour the house on several occasions before the sale was finalised so they'd been able to plot and plan and take measurements ahead of time.

Jack was moving through the house, blueprints in hand, double-checking everything, while Livia was in the kitchen with Sara making coffee.

'I can use all the help I can get,' said Livia. 'I've sorted through everything downstairs, and now I have to do the upstairs bedrooms yet. All those drawers and wardrobes ... I'll never buy a furnished house again!'

'You mentioned something about the attic,' Sara said. 'And I dreamed about it, can you believe it?'

Livia took out three coffee-mugs and spooned coffee crystals into them. 'With you, I believe anything. So what did you dream?'

'That we found a huge box of valuable antique jewellery.'

Livia laughed. 'They took her personal belongings out of the house, Sara. Her papers, jewellery, that sort of thing.'

'Maybe they didn't look in the attic. I can't wait to get up there and see what treasures are hidden there. Maybe a long-lost Van Gogh painting! Or maybe a Picasso! Just imagine! You'll be rich!'

Livia laughed and poured hot water into the mugs. 'Oh, be quiet, Sara! You read too many hidden treasure stories to your children. It's gone to your head.' Sara and Jack had two little girls and Sara loved reading to them.

'Well, it could happen, couldn't it? You hear about that sort of thing sometimes. This coffee is awful. Is it instant?'

'You were sitting here watching me make it. Of course it's instant.'

'So tell me about this guy.'

Livia told her about Clint Bracamonte. It felt good to be able to talk to somebody.

'Wow,' said Sara. 'Where is he going to live for the next couple of months?'

It wasn't what she'd expected Sara to say. 'I don't know. I don't care.'

Sara frowned, looking like a worried mother. 'You can't rent anything that short-term, you know. It's almost impossible. And he'll need a furnished place.'

'It's not my problem,' Livia said tightly.

'No, I know, I'm just thinking. He's in quite a bind.'

'I'm not responsible for his problems!'

Sara raised her brows. 'I didn't say that, but it must be quite a surprise to come back from overseas and find your home sold out from under you. No place to go. No bed to sleep in.'

'Oh, please, don't be melodramatic!'

Sara grinned. 'But I'm so good at it! How does it feel to have added to the homelessness statistic?'

Livia glared at her. 'The man has a ton of money in the bank, which, for all practical purposes, I put there personally. Don't ask me to feel sorry for him.'

Toys. A box of toy racing cars, a plastic bucket of Lego blocks, adventure books.

'These must be his,' Sara said, rummaging through the trunk.

'I suppose so.' Livia felt something pressing on her breastbone. She did not want to think of the big, rugged man as a little boy. A little boy playing with Lego blocks. A little boy visiting his grandmother in this house.

They'd crawled up a rickety pull-down ladder into the attic, fighting cobwebs and dust. Sara simply had to see what riches lay hidden in the dark there, and her enthusiasm had been contagious. A single small light bulb hung suspended from a wire, spreading a vague, dull light. Several pieces of old furniture, none of them precious antiques, languished in the dusty darkness. No paintings, famous or otherwise, revealed themselves. Instead of treasures, they found boxes and trunks full of old clothes and trinkets and draperies, and now they'd opened one full of toys. The trunk was newer than the others, just a cheap storage locker students took to college to keep their possessions in.

Sara kept pulling things out—a heap of typical boy toys lay spread out in front of them.

'Liv, look! A train set!' Sara said. 'It has everything! Mountains and tunnels and everything.' She looked up at Livia. 'This is worth money. What are you going to do with it?'

'I don't know,' she said tonelessly.

'You can't sell it, Liv. You'll have to give it back to him.'

'Yes.'

At every turn she was reminded how much the house belonged to him. His past was here. His memories. His damned toys!

*   *   *

Mrs Fletcher, the estate agent, drove up the drive in
her big shiny car as Jack and Sara were leaving late
that afternoon. The attic was empty. Tired of sorting
odds and ends, Sara and Livia had stripped the dining-
room of five layers of wallpaper. Jack had made
himself useful by cleaning out the gutters and digging
up a giant dead rhododendron bush. After that they'd
all carried the good pieces of furniture down to the
basement and covered them up for safe keeping. Livia
was exhausted.

'I have some interesting news for you!' Mrs Fletcher
said with a bright estate-agent smile. 'I have someone
who's interested in the house and wants to make a
deal.'

Alarms went off in her head. 'Let me guess,' she
said calmly. 'His name's Clint Bracamonte.'

Mrs Fletcher nodded. 'Yes. He mentioned you were
not interested in selling the house back to him as is.'

'That's right.' She wondered if Mrs Fletcher blamed
her, but she heard no censure in her tone. She imagined him going to his lawyer, trying to find a way
to get the house back. She wondered what he might
have said about her. She sighed. 'Come on in and I'll
make us some coffee.'

Mrs Fletcher followed her in. 'I told him he'd be
nuts to want it back the way it was because it needs
work and he'd end up having to deal with too many
repairs and other upkeep problems anyway and who's
going to deal with it once he's left the country again?
The place is going to fall apart.'

They sat on the back porch, the fragrance of lilacs
strong and sweet around them.

'What Mr Bracamonte suggested,' said Mrs Fletcher
after Livia had brought out two cups of coffee, 'was

an option to buy. He was willing to plunk down ten grand for that. Cash. I didn't think you'd go for it, though having ten thousand dollars as working capital must be a temptation.' She gave Livia a questioning look.

Livia nodded. 'Sure it is, but I don't want to sell an option. It means we have to set a sale price now and I don't feel I can do that reasonably yet. So much depends on the way the various jobs will go and how it all turns out. It's hard to tell what will happen.'

Mrs Fletcher nodded, stirring three spoons of sugar in her coffee. 'That's what I thought. And besides, with an option in his pocket, he's going to want his finger in the pie, making sure things are done a certain way. He's going to want to know what colour paint you're going to use and what quality tile in the bathroom and the kind of doorknobs on your doors, and so forth. Somehow I don't think you'll be able to work under those kind of conditions.'

Not in a hundred years. 'Right.' She would lose interest in the work very quickly. 'I want to do the job my way.' She *liked* her work. It was a real challenge to make the very best out of the house. And this house was special. She didn't want any interference.

'I made another suggestion,' said Mrs Fletcher. 'I told him he could offer to buy the right of first refusal. A thousand dollars is about standard.'

The right of first refusal. This meant that once the house was finished, she'd have to offer it to him before she put it on the market. Was there any reason not to?

Was there any reason why she shouldn't sell him the house once it was finished? After all, it didn't matter *who* bought the house.

'A thousand dollars is a thousand dollars,' said Mrs Fletcher practically. 'And you'll be free to determine the price the market will bear once it's finished and you won't be obliged to discuss any of the work with him. You'll be a free agent.'

'All right, you get the contract ready and I'll have a look at it.'

After Mrs Fletcher had left, Livia made herself some soup and crackers and went back to work. She put the train set and the other toys in the room Clint had slept in. She stared at his duffel bag, her stomach churning. She wanted him gone. Maybe signing a contract would get him out of the house.

It's the place I call home...

Just imagine coming home and finding your house has been sold out from under you...

Damn, damn! She hated feeling this way. As if she *owed* him something. As if she was guilty of something.

She lay awake for a long time that night, listening for his car, but it never came. Finally she fell into an exhausted sleep.

The next day she emptied one more bedroom and took up what seemed like miles of carpeting, listening all the time for his car, feeling nervous and jittery and hating herself for it.

Clint came back just after eight that evening. From the living-room window she saw him climb out of his car and her heart turned over. He looked like a different man. He wore new clothes—stone-coloured cotton trousers, navy jacket, a shirt and tie. His shoes gleamed with newness. His hair had been cut. Everything about him was crisp and streamlined—an image of professional confidence and authority. He even carried a leather briefcase. Very impressive.

She wasn't too impressive herself in her dirty jeans and T-shirt, but that was the way it went. She slipped back to the kitchen, feeling a breathless sense of trepidation. What would he think when he saw the house, which was now basically empty apart from his bedroom and one small room on the third floor?

'Hello, Livia.'

'Hi.' She felt tense all over. Brittle. Angry. 'The door has a bell,' she said coolly. 'Please use it.'

He ignored it, put the briefcase on the kitchen table and opened it. He extracted some papers. 'I have something for you to look at.'

She glanced at the papers. It wasn't difficult to see what it was. A contract for the right of first refusal.

'I understand Mrs Fletcher was here to discuss this with you yesterday afternoon.'

'Yes.' She glanced quickly over the paper. Then her eyes stopped. He intended to pay two thousand dollars. Cash, non-refundable. It was way more than the average fee. It was a very generous offer.

Her stomach churned. There was no reasonable way to refuse this deal. It was excellent business on her part to accept it. It would give her valuable cash up-front while she was doing all the work. And she was free to do what she wanted with the house.

But would she be? She bit her lip.

'Is something wrong?'

'No.' She swallowed. 'You're willing to pay a high fee.'

'I want to make sure you have no reason to refuse,' he said evenly.

She didn't. Not any reason that would make sense. Only reasons for which she had no words. Feelings, fears, apprehensions. And the damned little fairy jumping up and down inside her.

She collected herself. This was absurd. It was nothing more than a standard business agreement and the price was right. More than right. She sat down and began to read more carefully, making sure all was in order.

All was. It was a simple agreement, wrapped in legalistic jargon with which she was quite familiar by now.

'Do we have a deal?' He was still standing, looming over her, tall and commanding.

She met his eyes. 'It would be unreasonable to refuse it, wouldn't it?'

He gave a crooked smile. 'Yes, it would be,' he said quietly. There was something else in his voice, something beyond the calm tone. Anxiety plucked at her insides.

'And if I want to be unreasonable?' she asked.

He leaned towards her, bracing his hands on the table, his face close to hers. 'Then so will I.' There was a devilish gleam in his black eyes. 'I will haunt you, sweet Olivia. One way or another I will own this house again, don't doubt it for a moment.'

She didn't. Once she was done with it it would be up for sale. Anybody with money could buy it. She shrugged. 'I don't doubt it.' He was so close that she could smell the warm male scent of him. It had a disastrous effect on her heart rate.

He straightened, and tapped the document with a brown finger. 'You sign this and I'll get my things and be gone.' Pushing his jacket back, he slipped his hands in his trouser pockets and observed her calmly, waiting for a reply.

'Where will you go?' she asked. It came out automatically and she regretted the words instantly. She didn't care where he went. She didn't even want to know.

It's the place I call home ... His words echoed in her head.

He shrugged his broad shoulders. 'A hotel, a motel, whatever. Would you prefer to sign this in front of a witness or a notary public? Or are you comfortable with just the two of us doing it right here?'

The two of us. It was not at all a comfortable concept. It sounded way too intimate. However, signing the contract here didn't make it any less of a binding document.

'Show me your money and I'll sign it.'

He laughed. It was a warm, rich sound that slipped straight into her bloodstream. He went over to the briefcase, took out a cheque-book and began to write. Then he handed her the cheque.

She studied it. His name was on it, as well as his address. The address was the house the two of them were sitting in. His grandmother's house. The house he called home. The house she now owned. She felt another pang of unreasonable guilt.

'Thank you.' She picked up a pen and signed the contract and handed it to him. He signed it too. She watched his hand as the pen moved with large, bold strokes to write his name. They both signed another copy.

'All done.' He straightened and extended his hand. 'Now we shake hands.'

What could she do but extend hers? His grip was warm and firm and sent sparks of fire flying through her blood. His eyes looked straight into hers. 'Thank you,' he said.

She extracted her hand, afraid if he held hers any longer she would start to glow like a bonfire. 'You're welcome,' she said in her best business voice.

He took his briefcase and went upstairs. He came down again only minutes later.

'I found the toys and the train set you put in my room,' he said. 'I'll make you an offer, if you like.'

She clenched her hands. 'Oh, for God's sake, just take them! They're yours, aren't they?'

'They *used* to be mine,' he said calmly. 'And that train set is quite valuable. It used to belong to my father. Now, however, it's all yours, Olivia, as you've pointed out before.'

Was he tormenting her on purpose? Showing how wrong it all was for her to own his house, his childhood toys, his memories?

She shrugged. 'So it's mine. That means I can do with it as I please. So I'm giving them to you. Free of charge. How's that?'

'You're very generous.'

'Oh, stop it!' she said irritably, and turned her back on him. It had nothing to do with being generous, had it?

She felt his hand on her shoulder. 'What's the matter, Olivia? Are you angry?'

She shrugged off his hand. He'd touched her only lightly, yet it had felt like being touched by a live wire. 'No, I'm not angry!' His face was very close, his eyes locking hers. She couldn't breathe. The silence thundered in her ears.

What is wrong with me? she asked herself. Why am I feeling this way? No man had ever had this effect on her and it was terrifying. She stepped back slowly, taking in a careful breath, still looking into his eyes, incapable of breaking the contact.

Something flickered briefly in his dark eyes, then he reached up and raked his hand through his hair. 'All right,' he said roughly, 'I'll go up and get that stuff in my car.'

She fled into the living-room and began to scrape old flaking paint from the window-frame. She heard him move up and down the stairs and watched through the window as he carried the boxes of toys out and put them in the trunk of his car.

Her heart clenched tight. She was staring at the window-sill, seeing nothing, hearing Sara's voice. Imagine coming home and finding your house sold out from under you...

He strode back in the house, up the stairs, then down again. Her legs seemed made of wood. She moved awkwardly out of the room into the entry-way. He had his duffel bag in his hand and he stopped in front of her.

They looked at each other, saying nothing, and her throat went dry. She swallowed with difficulty. Looking into his black eyes, she felt as if she were falling into some deep dark hole—falling and falling and never reaching the bottom.

'Olivia?' he said softly.

She moistened her dry lips. 'As long as you're going to buy the house back from me,' she heard herself say, 'you might as well stay here.'

CHAPTER FOUR

SILENCE vibrated between them, broken by the sudden creaking of the wooden floor beneath his feet.

'Are you sure?' Clint asked quietly.

'This is your home. You need a place to stay.'

'You don't owe me, Olivia.'

No, she did not owe him. So why then did she feel as if she did? And was that the reason she'd invited him to stay? Or was something else involved? Was it her attraction to him? To that irresistible magnetism of him?

A dark flame flickered in his eyes. 'Do you think it would be wise?' he asked softly. 'The two of us alone in this house?'

The air was suddenly charged. Her heart began to throb and her throat went dry. She couldn't tear her gaze away from his eyes. She swallowed hard. 'I don't know,' she said, 'would it be?'

The question hung between them, and the air was alive with tension.

'I'll be gone in two months,' he said then, his voice very quiet. It was more than a simple statement. It was a warning: I'll be gone in two months. Alone.

Recklessness overwhelmed her. 'I know that.' Fear clutched at her heart. She felt in the grip of a wild and dangerous insanity and she couldn't stop herself. Did not want to stop herself.

He took her hand, smiling faintly. 'Then I would like nothing better.'

*　　*　　*

Livia had set up office in the small den off the front entrance. A sheet of plywood over two sawhorses served as a large desk. There was a phone and a couple of chairs. Stacks of catalogues, construction manuals, design books, piles of colour samples, paint samples, fabric samples and everything else she needed were neatly organised along the wall and on the desk.

She sat at the plywood desk, coffee at her side, and stared at the blueprints spread out in front of her. It was just past six in the morning and she hadn't slept all night. No, not true. She had slept for a while. And while she had slept she had dreamed.

The dream had been so exciting, so wonderful, and, in the end, so sad that she'd woken up crying.

And after that she'd not been able to sleep again.

Doom had settled in the darkness around her, filling the bedroom with fear and apprehension. Outside, an owl had hooted in the woods and it had given her the shivers.

Finally, with the first tentative chirps of bird song, she'd crawled out of her sleeping-bag, pulled on some clothes and made the coffee. So here she was, drinking coffee, waiting for the light to chase away darkness and doom from the house, from her heart.

But the first part of the dream had been nice. So nice in fact that the mere thought of it made her feel warm all over. Well, maybe it was the coffee. It was a bit chilly yet so early in the morning.

She took another gulp of coffee and focused her eyes on the blueprint. Tomorrow the contractor would come for stage one of the renovation: demolition.

Destruction: broken walls, pieces of timber, plaster, dust and more dust, and the most godawful mess you'd ever see. It was the most exciting part of the job. She loved it. So, why was she sitting here, not feeling excited at all?

At six-thirty he came down in running shorts and went out. He was bare-chested and she watched him from the office window, her heart in her throat. He had powerful legs and shoulders and his body moved with sleek animal grace. After last night's dream this was not what she needed. She turned away, annoyed at the way he affected her, at the way her pulse leaped at the sight of him.

She was emptying kitchen cabinets, sorting through pots and pans and baking dishes when he came back forty-five minutes later.

'Good morning,' he said, taking in the crowded counters and cardboard boxes filled with kitchen things. He made no comment, but reached for a glass and filled it under the tap. He was shiny with sweat, all primal male strength and beauty, and her senses jumped to full alert. She watched him gulp down the water, his head thrown back.

His glass empty, he reached for the tap, then suddenly lowered his hand slowly as if reconsidering. He stood very still, his eyes riveted on the jumble on the counter. For an endless moment he did not move, he just stood there staring, an expression on his face she could not read. Livia's heart made a nervous little leap.

'Clint? Is something wrong?' she asked. 'Are you all right?'

He turned his face to look at her, but it seemed his eyes did not see her. They were far away in some other place and time. He shook his head as if to shake something away. 'I'm fine,' he said, but his voice sounded dull and dead. He refilled his glass and took it outside to the porch.

She watched his back, then came to her feet. Her left leg was asleep and tingled painfully. She'd been sitting on it wrong. Standing in front of the sink, she surveyed the stacks of mismatched plates and dishes and cups on the counter. What was it that he had seen there? Nothing unusual caught her eye.

She went on with her work, but her mind wouldn't leave the incident alone. She picked up a rubbish bag full of discarded items and carried it out to the skip. He was standing at the porch railing and stared off into the greenery.

'Shall I fix some breakfast now?' she asked.

'I'd better have a shower first,' he said, and gave her a half-smile.

'All right, sure.' She went back inside, glancing again at the counter, wondering what he had seen there. She shrugged irritably, then went back outside.

'Clint?'

'Yes?'

'I'm going through all that stuff in the kitchen. I'm throwing the old things out and before I go on I thought I'd ask you if there's anything in particular you want to keep.'

'No.' He didn't look at her.

She stared at the back of his head. His hair curled damply around his ears.

Her pulse quickened. 'You saw something. You were looking at something a few minutes ago.'

His head whipped back to look at her. 'I told you no,' he said tightly. 'Just get rid of the stuff; I don't want it.'

But she didn't get rid of everything. Some of the things she kept simply for their own use while living in the house. The rest of the good, usable items she packed in boxes and stored them in the basement. If he was going to buy the house back, he'd probably want the kitchen stocked with the basic equipment. She could put it back after the kitchen had been remodelled.

She gave an aggravated sigh. Why was she thinking of him? Why did he seem to enter into everything she did?

'I assume you have drawings for the remodelling?' he asked over dinner that night. He had left that morning after a quick breakfast and he'd been gone all day, wearing another set of impeccable clothes. Despite the formal, well-cut business clothes, there was no doubt as to the rugged physical strength of the body beneath.

She stared at his tie, feeling her body tense at his question. 'Yes, of course.'

'I'd like to see them.'

Oh, would he, now? She felt herself bristle. He wasn't asking, he was demanding. It was there in his voice, the way he looked at her.

He wiped his mouth with a napkin and took a drink from his wine. 'I want to know what you're intending to do to this house. Is it too much to ask?'

She supposed not, yet she resented his proprietorial tone. He had no rights, no rights at all. She did not have to explain or defend. She took a bite of warmed-up frozen lasagne.

Yet if she refused to show him, she would appear to be unreasonable and petty. And he would find a way to see them anyway. All he had to do was go into her office when she wasn't around.

So she gathered her pride and composure. 'They're in my office. I'll show you after dinner.' How calm she sounded! How reasonable.

What if he didn't like a sun-room off the living-room? What if he didn't want the kitchen enlarged? What if he didn't want a large bathroom with a whirlpool upstairs?

Easy, she said to herself. If he doesn't like it, he doesn't have to buy the house.

Only it wasn't so easy, and she knew it. Everything had changed and it made her angry and defensive. She had so looked forward to this job, and it seemed now that the shine had gone off it. With every turn she made he was there, in her thoughts, in her considerations, in the very things she found in the house. In her damned dreams!

Dinner over, they went into her office and she unfolded the drawings and spread them out on the desk. Hands in his pockets, he stood beside her, towering over her. She smelled aftershave. Her heart-rate quickened.

'Here,' she said, pointing at the kitchen. 'This is the way it's going to be.' And she started talking, explaining, pointing.

The kitchen would be gutted, the wall that separated it from the little breakfast-room would be torn down. The outside living-room wall would go to open it up to a sun-room that would be added.

As she talked, enthusiasm took over her anger. He asked questions; she explained. She talked and talked, feeling herself grow warm with excitement, because after all this was a challenging job, more challenging than the others she'd done before. But she felt up to it, and she was certain, in the depths of her soul, that it would be a success, that the house would be absolutely wonderful.

She gestured, pointed, and then his hand was touching hers on the drawing and it was like a shockwave going through her. Her voice faltered for a moment, then with every ounce of will-power she went on talking.

'I'm not changing the style and character of the house, you see. I'd never do that It's country colonial and I wouldn't want to make it look like a California contemporary.' She heard herself talk, heard the tone of her voice, and she knew that what she was doing, ever so subtly, was asking for his approval.

His fingers curled around hers on the drawing, gently, lightly. She could slide her hand away, escape his fingers, but she had no power. She was mesmerised by his hands, the feel of his fingers.

She stopped talking. And the silence was electric. The blood pounded in her ears. She looked at their hands entwined, feeling his gaze on her. Slowly she lifted her face to his, meeting his eyes, and her heart lurched.

It was no secret what was in those dark eyes and it shouldn't shock her so, yet it did. It shouldn't shock her because she saw her own feelings reflected there—the same hunger, the same yearning. She felt his hands slide up her arms, slowly, sensuously, sliding over her shoulders up to cup her face.

His gaze drifted down to her mouth. 'I think,' he said softly, 'it will be perfect.'

His mouth was close, so close. She felt the warmth of his breath on her skin. She closed her eyes and his lips touched hers—just touched with a featherlike, tantalising gentleness. Then his mouth closed over hers and there was magic—a mingling of strength and gentleness, and his tongue doing an erotic little dance with hers.

A soft moan escaped her and his kiss intensified, pulsing now with deeper need until she felt dizzy with it. Her legs were trembling and she put her arms around him to steady herself. His back was hard and strong under her hands and the warmth coming through his shirt seemed to flow over into her.

They pulled away at the same time. His hands gently released her head and wandered down her shoulders and arms. He took a step back, a faint smile softening the hard, taut lines of his face.

'A dangerous game, this,' he said softly.

Nothing seemed quite the same after that. There was a subtle change in the atmosphere between them—a sense of waiting, a sense of nervous apprehension.

Most days he was gone during the day, lecturing or giving presentations, but the moment he stepped into the house the tensions were back and the air seemed to crackle between them.

He did not kiss or even touch her again, yet the memory of that first time hung like a presence between them. She was acutely aware of his eyes following her every move, watching her as if he were looking for clues or secrets. She had no secrets, nothing worth this relentless scrutiny.

When they had a meal together she invariably talked too much, out of sheer nerves. Silence frightened her and so, as she filled the silent spaces with words, she told him everything about herself. He seemed not to mind her chatter, even seemed amused now and then.

'You have a very sexy voice,' he said one day, making her heart turn over. But it didn't make her stop talking. She asked questions, too many questions. He didn't answer all of them, but he did some.

He'd grown up with his parents in Richmond, but they'd died in a ferry accident during his first year in college. So during the holidays he'd stay with his grandmother. He had no other close family.

She could not imagine it. She had scores of family—aunts, uncles, cousins. To be alone in the world like this seemed awful. Yet he certainly did not elicit her pity. He was not the kind of man who'd take kindly to her showing him pity, either.

He was a man who took his work seriously, and she listened with rapt attention as he told her of his life in the forest, and how traditional lives were changing with the lumber companies driving further and further inland destroying the forests. His research involved studying traditional communities and the way people used their forest environment—the plants, wood, fungi, insects and other forest products they used for food, medicines, tools and utensils.

He was not alone, as she had initially assumed, but worked together with another American scientist, David Holloway, a botanist.

The village was tiny, hidden deep in the interior, and could only be reached on foot. One enormous longhouse sheltered all one hundred and three villagers. A longhouse, she knew, was a large structure built off the forest ground on hardwood poles. Along the wide veranda that stretched the length of the building, many doors led into the private family rooms.

He told her of the people in the longhouse village with genuine liking and respect. He played games with the children and knew all of them by name.

Little by little she glimpsed what lay behind the dark eyes—a compassionate, caring nature—and she liked what she saw.

She loved listening to him talk. Fascinated by his stories, she would forget everything around her. Then something would happen—a look, an accidental touch, and all would be forgotten and what she saw was only him. The stranger who had invaded her house had invaded her heart as well.

She knew she loved him.

All she could think of as she worked on the house was him. Feverish, passionate imaginings haunted her dreams.

He was gone for several days, lecturing in New York and Philadelphia. He would spend the weekend with friends and wouldn't be back until Monday.

While the workmen were doing their manly thing with sledgehammers, Livia was in the third-floor bedroom, taking down curtains and going through the wardrobe and dresser. There wasn't much there—a sewing machine, sewing supplies, patterns and some lengths of material. And then at the bottom of a deep drawer she found the dress. A tiny party dress for a tiny girl, yellow with white daisies hand-embroidered on the bodice and white lace along the tiny collar. It was all finished apart from the hem. It was a lovely little dress. Had the old lady been sewing this and not had time to finish?

What little girl was meant to have it? Yet it had seemed hidden at the bottom of that drawer as if abandoned. It looked as if it had been there for a long time and it had the vaguely musty smell of something damp and un-aired.

She held it up and smiled. It could be washed and hemmed. She might find someone to give it to. She put it aside and went on piling old patterns and scraps of material into the plastic rubbish bag.

She was glad Clint was gone for the next three days. It gave her breathing space. Every time she looked at him she'd practically start trembling. How could any man have such an effect on her? She kept thinking of the dream and fear would overwhelm her. What was she getting herself into? Would she be able to be rational about it? Would she be able to handle it like a grown-up, mature adult woman?

She groaned. She didn't feel like a grown-up, mature adult woman. She felt out of control, wild with hunger. It was embarrassing. She wanted to dance in the grass in her bare feet. She wanted to laugh. So she laughed.

It sounded rather strange, so she stopped. People who laughed out loud to themselves in empty houses might be suspected of having a mental condition.

Maybe she had. She grinned to herself. Maybe love was a mental condition.

It was Sunday afternoon and the silence was bliss. The workmen were gone. No sledgehammers, no saws, no voices, no portable tape decks wailing country music. She was alone, completely alone, and she wanted to enjoy the peace while it lasted. Tomorrow Clint would be back.

The sun was shining and it was a perfect spring day, the temperature mild, a soft breeze stirring the new greenery and the air full of the scent of roses. Livia took a large towel and went outside. She was going to lie down in the grass and soak up the sun. She deserved a little rest and relaxation, and communion with nature was good for the soul. The grass was cool under her bare feet. She'd spent so much time inside, it felt like paradise to be out. It was paradise. She lifted her face to the sun and smiled.

She found a perfect spot in the sun and spread out the towel. It was so quiet. Only the birds and the hum of a bee broke the silence. She was alone in paradise.

She laughed, and then, on impulse, she stripped off her shorts, T-shirt and her silky scraps of frivolous underthings and stretched her arms to the blue sky overhead. It felt great! Then she lay down on the towel and closed her eyes. Ah, bliss! Maybe in one of her earlier lives she had lived on a tropical island where people wore no clothes. It was a wonderfully free feeling. The soft spring air was like velvet on her skin, the sunlight warm and sensuous. She took in a deep breath and smelled the scent of grass and clover and warm earth.

Something awoke her from her slumber. Something tickled. An ant crawling up her arm. She kept her eyes closed as she moved a lazy hand along her arm. She felt weightless. She didn't want to move. It felt so good lying here in the sun, dozing, her body languid and warm.

She sensed movement by her side and her eyes flew open in sudden alarm.

Clint. Her heart lurched, then set off in a gallop of trepidation. He was barefoot, bare-chested and

wore only a pair of khaki shorts, and he was sitting
next to her in the grass, looking at her.

She lay there, transfixed by that broad chest, those
smouldering eyes and she couldn't move.

'Clint...' she said, but it was only a breath of air,
less than a whisper. The fear was gone, replaced by
another emotion—a need, a terrible yearning.

'Yes,' he said.

She felt her body bloom under his regard, a feeling
so luscious, so natural that nothing could stop it. I
love him, she thought.

'You're so beautiful,' he said softly, smiling faintly
into her eyes. 'Do you mind my looking at you?'

'No,' she whispered back. She did not mind. It did
not feel wrong. With any other man it would have
been wrong, but not with Clint, not here. Her body
felt rich and ripe, the sun warm on her skin.

He laid a hand on her cheek. 'You feel warm.'

The contact sparkled her blood and she wanted to
give in to the delicious feeling, yet reason stirred.

'We can't,' she whispered. 'We...'

'Yes, we can,' he whispered back. 'I knew.'

It was difficult to breathe. 'You knew what?'

'I saw you from my bedroom window. I knew...I
wanted you.' He trailed his hand down her throat with
tantalising sensuality. 'I wouldn't have come down
here to find you without...thinking.' He gave a faint
smile. 'I've wanted you for a long time, Livia.'

'Yes,' she whispered, dizzy with the touch of his
eyes, the sound of his voice. It was inevitable that this
should happen. She'd known it since the first time
she'd seen him. It had hovered between them in the
air, it had danced through her blood, tingled under
her skin, haunted her in her dreams.

He smiled down at her, his dark eyes full of a smouldering fire ready to burst into flame. He touched his finger to her mouth, a fluttering of warmth.

'Do you want me, gypsy woman?' he asked softly.

CHAPTER FIVE

A BLACK lock of hair fell over Clint's forehead. The corners of his eyes crinkled as he smiled into her eyes with sensuous invitation. The smile softened the angular, rugged lines of his face. His teeth were bright against the dark tan.

Livia wanted to touch him, run her finger along the contours of his mouth. She wanted to feel his lips on hers, and on all the rest of her body. And she had wanted it for a long time.

'Yes,' she whispered, reaching out for his hand and putting it on her breast. She saw the tremor running through him.

'Every time I look at you, I go crazy inside,' he said on a low note. His chest rose and fell rapidly with each breath. 'There's something generous and loving about you that shines in your eyes and gets to my gut every time.'

'So why did it take you so long?' she whispered.

'I'm a man of great self-restraint,' he said with faint self-derision. He fondled her breast with gentle, erotic little touches. 'And why didn't you seduce me?' he asked then.

'I'm a woman of great self-restraint,' she said promptly. 'And will you please kiss me now?'

He did. His mouth made her blood sing and her skin tingle. He took off his clothes and lay on his side beside her and made magic with his hands and mouth.

'You are so beautiful,' he said huskily. 'You feel so soft and warm and sexy.'

She drank in the words with feverish delight, reaching out to touch him, eager to feel every inch of his strong, muscled body, so different from her own, so wonderfully enticing.

The scent of clover and crushed grass wafted around them. She closed her eyes against the brightness of the azure sky and turned on her side to press herself against him, restless and full of longing for more.

His chest was rising and falling rapidly and she rested her mouth against the warm skin, the curly hair tickling her face. He smelled wonderfully male, a clean, exciting scent that filled her head and made her warm and dizzy. She felt the throbbing of his heart, and that of her own, and was gripped by a sweet delirium.

He was in her arms, this big dark stranger she'd fallen in love with, and he wanted her.

Oh, how he wanted her! His mouth, his hands and all the rest of his body told her so. And she wanted him back with a deep and honest need because in the past weeks he had wrapped himself around her heart and she knew he belonged there forever. He was the most wonderful sexy man she had ever met and she loved his dark, secretive eyes, and one day she would know everything.

He made love to her in a slow, sensual way, tantalising her until she thought she'd go mad. Her body pulsed and quivered, and she moaned against his mouth, and then it was no longer slow and gentle, but full of fire and passion. She gave him back in full measure, savouring the feel and taste of him, the strength of his body, hard and soft at the same time.

No restraint now. No inhibitions or thoughts or questions. Her body sang, her senses danced and all was magic.

A bee droned near by and the soft summer breeze stroked her heated skin. They were outside in the grass, under a blue summer sky, and nothing could have been more right.

It was better than her dreams, better than her wildest fantasies, because this was real.

She whispered his name. In answer his body shuddered against her and instantly the aching tension inside her broke into waves of rapturous release.

Breathless, they clung together, languor slowly taking over their sated bodies. His warm mouth nuzzled her neck.

'You're wonderful,' he murmured.

'I was...wild,' she whispered back, faintly embarrassed by her own abandon. Her hands rested on the back of his head, her fingers curling through his damp hair.

He chuckled. 'A true gypsy woman—wild and passionate. That doesn't bother you, I hope?'

'No, no...I just didn't know I could ever feel quite so totally wanton.'

'And did you like feeling so totally wanton?'

'Yes,' she admitted. It was quite a wonderful feeling to just let go. 'And you're quite wild yourself, may I point out, for someone with so much self-restraint?'

He laughed softly. 'When I let go of the restraint, there's no telling what will happen.' He kissed her gently and wiped a strand of hair away from her cheek. 'This was quite wonderful, out here under the sky.'

'Yes. Like a fantasy. I didn't expect you to come back today. And then when I woke up, there you were.' She smiled. 'I've been having fantasies about you,' she added.

'And I about you.'

'Really?' she asked.

'Don't tell me you didn't know. You must have known.'

'I was hoping,' she admitted, and closed her eyes, smiling. 'I'm so... I don't know the word. Sated. Fulfilled. Worn out. I don't think I'll be able to move for hours.'

'We can stay here. We can have a picnic dinner with wine and cheese and peaches and sleep under the stars.'

Her eyes flew open. 'Oh, that would be great!'

And so they did. They drank wine and ate cheese and peaches while fire flies glowed in the dark. They made love again and slept under the stars.

In the morning they awoke in each other's arms to the sweet warble of a single bird, a joyful song more beautiful than any music.

'It must be a love song,' he whispered, and they made love again.

The weeks that followed were bliss. Livia had never been happier in her life. Clint was an attentive and passionate lover, enjoying her advances when she made them.

Little by little she carefully drew him into the work, asking him about his preferences in terms of colour and style. It was a secret delight to find their tastes did not differ much. However, it was rather obvious that house decorating was not one of his burning passions, and he seemed perfectly happy to let her do her thing. He showed no desire to interfere with her work in any way, or to put forward his own ideas and demand they be implemented.

She started fantasising about living together in the house, taking trips together to exotic places. She would help him with his research or come up with projects of her own. She was a fair photographer; maybe she could become a really good one. She'd take stunning pictures, have them published, win prizes, become famous. If you dreamed, you might as well dream big. She would smile at her own fantasies as she hammered away installing extra shelving in a cupboard, or painted window trims.

'Why aren't you married?' he asked one night, his face nestled between her breasts.

It was a good question. 'Men are scared of me,' she said.

He laughed, lifting his face to look at her. 'What do you expect? You beat them at their own games. You drive a pick-up truck. You know how to handle he-man tools. You crawl on top of roofs and fix leaks. On top of all that you are a successful business-woman and when they touch you you use karate on them. Very intimidating, Livia.'

Only he wasn't intimidated. He was amused.

'So what am I supposed to do? Pretend I'm a helpless, simpering female so they can feel macho and needed?'

'Not for me you don't have to.'

'But then you're not intimidated,' she said, sliding her fingers through the thickness of his hair.

'True. I'm fascinated.'

'Oh, really?'

'Yes. I find it fascinating to see you run around in jeans wielding hammer and saw and then at night you've got your hair down, wearing a soft sexy nightgown and you smell of jasmine. So sexy, so tempting.'

'I'm glad you find me sexy and tempting, because I also find you very sexy and tempting.'

'It's a very convenient coincidence.'

'Coincidence? How can you call this coincidence?' She nipped at his earlobe. 'It's providence, fate, kismet.'

He silenced her with a kiss.

That afternoon, a large flower arrangement was delivered by a Charlottesville florist. 'For the sexiest carpenter around,' the card read. Clint had signed it himself.

She put the bouquet on a stool in the middle of the empty living-room and left the door open so she could see it every time she passed.

The work was going well. The sun-room had been built, the new bathroom and the whirlpool installed, as had the central air-conditioning. The kitchen was almost finished. The electricians and plumbers and various other workers had departed, and the house was blissfully silent again. Now came the painting, the floor work, and a host of other detail work.

One day she was painting a bedroom cupboard, doing acrobatic contortions to reach the corners in the small space, when Clint came into the room.

'Look what I found outside,' he said.

She untangled herself, sat down on her knees, blew hair out of her face and held the paintbrush over the can. She looked at his hand.

In it squirmed and chirped the tiniest naked little baby bird she had ever seen.

'Oh, my,' she whispered, 'that poor little thing.' She was whispering, as if even the sound of her voice would hurt the delicate, vulnerable creature.

Clint's big hand curved protectively around the tiny bird. 'I found him under the big hickory tree in the back. I don't see a nest, but he must have fallen out of one.'

'He has only barely hatched; he doesn't even have feathers yet. He's not going to make it.'

Clint gave a light shrug. 'I couldn't just let him lie there, screeching his little heart out. Do you have an eye dropper?'

She met his eyes. 'Are you going to try and save it?'

'What choice do we have?'

Well, not any she could think of.

So they tried to save the pitiful bird. In an old shoebox Clint made a nest with grass and paper tissue. He bought a book about rescuing various kinds of wildlife. They pored over it together. They scrutinised the tiny creature, trying to determine what kind of bird it was.

'Maybe it's a cardinal,' she said, thinking of the bright red bird it would be when it would mature, at least if it were a male. 'Or a robin or bluebird.'

They fed it every two hours—milk from an eye dropper, tiny bits of raw ground beef, mashed-up hard-boiled egg. In the mornings his frantic screeching reached all the way up to the bedroom.

It lived. Every day it seemed to chirp louder and louder. It grew. It began to grow feathers.

It was not a cardinal, nor a bluebird, nor a red-breasted robin. It was a sparrow—mousy brown, plain.

They watched it as it perched on Clint's index finger, flapping its wings, chirping frantically, desperate to fly.

'It's life,' Clint said, smiling at the tiny, fluttering creature.

Livia looked at the big man and the tiny bird and felt her heart flow over with love.

They spent a lot of time talking. Livia liked talking. She enjoyed figuring people out, what their background was, what they cared about, why they had the job they did. For obvious reasons she was more than a little interested in Clint, but Clint was not all that forthcoming about himself, except when it concerned his job.

He loved his work in the rainforest and it was obvious he was anxious to get back to Kalimantan. The project would last another two years, studying several more traditional longhouse communities. After that he planned to come back, teach for a while and probably go overseas again for another project.

She tried not to think about Clint leaving. But slowly, insidiously, fear crept into her mind. Had she been stupid to let things get this far? Stupid to hope he might change his mind?

Was she imagining something that was not there? In his eyes, his touch, his lovemaking?

He never spoke about her joining him. It was obvious she was not part of his future. He'd made no promises.

'I'll be gone in two months,' he had said.

*   *   *

The whirlpool bath was big enough for two. When she'd planned its installation she'd never in her wildest dreams imagined herself in it with a man. At the time there had been no man in her life. Now there was Clint and sitting in the whirlpool together was a nice way to finish the day, to soothe her muscles and relax. A glass of wine also helped.

He'd been gone for three days lecturing in New York, and he had suggested they try out the bath.

'I want to know if it works,' he'd said, giving her a devilish look.

It worked. It was wonderful. It was relaxing. It was exciting.

Later, they made slow, sensuous love on the big bed, and afterwards she lay nestled in his arms, her back against his firm chest, their legs entwined, wondering how this could possibly ever end. They fitted together perfectly. They belonged together. For ever and ever.

He was leaving in two weeks.

When the house was finished, she could follow him. Stay with him in the rainforest village. Wherever he was she wanted to be. She was a gypsy; she had an adventurous spirit. It was so simple.

She stroked his hand that lay flat on her stomach. 'You realise that I'll be done with the house in about six weeks?' she murmured.

'It's been going faster than you had estimated, then?'

'Yes. It's because I'm inspired. Having you around is doing wonders for my energy level.'

He chuckled. 'I've noticed.' He nuzzled her neck. 'So what are you going to do when the house is finished?' he asked lazily.

A simple question, asked in a tone that indicated he was not involved with the issue. By then he would be gone and they would no longer be together.

Maybe she'd misunderstood his tone. Maybe he was interested to find out if she was open to other possibilities. Maybe he really didn't know how she felt.

She went on stroking his hand. 'I'm going to roam the world and search for adventure,' she said lightly. 'My gypsy blood is stirring. It always does between houses.' In the last few years she had spent time biking through Europe, safari-ing through Kenya and sailing in the Caribbean. This time she had planned to explore the Amazon rainforest, or rather a portion thereof. However, amazingly, she had suddenly found that the rainforest of Borneo held even more appeal. She'd neglected to make any necessary arrangements for her intended trip to Brazil.

He was winding a strand of her hair around his finger. 'And where will you go?'

'I'll climb mountains and traverse deserts,' she said, speaking lightly again, but her heart was beating faster. 'Then I'll come to Kalimantan and see how you're doing all alone in the deep dark forest.' Oh, God, what was she doing? What was she saying?

'A terrible idea,' he said, equally lightly. 'You'd get lost before you found me. You'd get chewed up by leeches and bitten by spiders and you'd have to eat smoked boar and bee-larvae soup.'

'You're trying to scare me off,' she said, pseudowounded. 'I'm very strong and very smart. I even speak Bahasa Indonesia, remember? I'd get myself some guides and rent a boat. Sooner or later I'd get there.'

'After the river becomes impassable, you'll have to walk for two days.' His voice was even, yet she could feel the tension in his body as it touched hers. He had stopped playing with her hair.

'I can walk and I so like adventure,' she whispered.

'You won't like leeches crawling up your legs.' He turned her on her back, leaning over her, looking into her eyes. 'Go on your trip. See Java again, hang out on the beach on Bali, but don't venture into the Kalimantan forest. It's too damned dangerous.'

She should stop right there. Let it go. But she was not good at giving up and a streak of stubbornness had often served her well.

'I'm tough. And I'd love to visit a longhouse village and see how you live,' she said recklessly, knowing she was in deep water now. Knowing she'd ignored all the warning signs. 'It might be very interesting.' She smiled brightly. 'I could stay for a while and learn how to weave mats or make traditional medicine, or I could bring a tape recorder and record people telling me traditional stories and myths. Then I'd have them translated, publish them and become very rich. What do you think of that idea?'

He faced her silently. She sensed the terrible tension in him and her heart began to gallop.

'I think,' he said slowly, 'that you've got the wrong idea, Livia.' He turned away from her, got off the bed and went into the bathroom. She heard the shower.

She listened to the rush of water, her heart turning to stone.

He had warned her. She'd gone into this with her eyes wide open, but she had dreamed like a silly woman, hoping that his love for her would win over his reservations, would make him see that he could not live without her. She was such a romantic. She believed in love and romance and all that was good and lovely and wonderful. It was naïve, and at her age she should know better.

The shower was turned off, and a few minutes later Clint emerged from the bathroom, a towel wrapped around his hips, his hair damp. He sat down on the bed at her side and took her hand.

'I didn't mean to mislead you, Livia,' he said softly.

She willed herself to be calm. She looked into his face and took in a deep, steadying breath. 'You didn't. I misled myself.'

He glanced down at their hands together on the sheet. 'Permanence is not for me.' His voice was rough. 'My kind of life does not lend itself to marriage.'

'I understand,' she said. She was, after all, a reasonable person.

'I'm sorry if you're hurt.'

'I'll get over it.' It was a lie. She did not think she would ever get over it. But she did have her pride and her dignity. She would not fall to pieces in front of him. It was all her own fault. He had warned her.

I'll be gone in two months...

She had disregarded that warning, had assumed that once he loved her he would not be able to let her go from his life. She'd assumed that she would show him true love, that once he understood the power of it, he would not let go of her.

She had been wrong. She had failed. In the end all that they'd had was a short affair—beautiful on the outside, empty on the inside. Now she would have to live with the consequences.

'You deserve happiness, Livia. You are a warm, loving, exciting woman and you deserve a man who can give you what you need. But I'm not that man.'

He didn't love her. He had never intended to love her. He had intended to leave her and he had told her so. She withdrew her hand and sat upright, pulling the sheet up with her. She would not have covered her breasts earlier this evening, or yesterday or the day before. Now she did, and as he looked at her she knew that the gesture had not escaped him.

His eyes met hers. 'I didn't mean to hurt you, Livia. I thought you understood.'

She bit her lip. 'I did. I thought I could . . . handle it. I was wrong. It's my own mistake and I take full responsibility.' It sounded so mature, so together. But she didn't feel mature and together. She wanted to scream, break down in tears. Instead, she smiled bravely. 'Don't worry. I'm not going to fall to pieces and make a scene.'

His face worked. His eyes glowed dark and wild and he cursed under his breath. He rose abruptly and turned his back on her, every muscle in his body hard as steel.

'There's no reason to be angry,' she said, her voice shaking a little.

'Dammit, there is!' The words cracked like an explosion. 'There's every damned reason to be angry! I didn't want to hurt you! I shouldn't have let this happen!'

She stared at his brown back. 'I don't think it was a matter of *letting* it happen,' she said huskily. 'It just did.' She paused. 'And it wasn't just you, you know. I was there too. And you weren't in charge of me or my actions or my feelings, so don't act as if you had any control over all of this.'

He turned, his black gaze meeting hers. 'I should have seen it coming. All the signs were there.'

All the signs of what? That she loved him? Well, she wasn't good at keeping secrets. Her heart ached. She loved him, and he didn't love her. It was simple, devastatingly simple.

She slipped out of bed. Her hands were shaking as she put on a robe. She moved to the door and opened it. 'I'll get my things out of here tomorrow.'

'Livia . . .' It was an oddly strangled sound. 'Please, don't do this.'

Her hand clasped the doorknob hard. She straightened her back and met his eyes. 'I have to. I . . . I can't handle it any other way.' Anguish almost overwhelmed her. 'I'm not sophisticated enough for a detached affair.' She turned and walked out the door.

His car was gone by the time she got up the next morning, bleary-eyed from lack of sleep. She was supposed to be painting, but she didn't have the energy. Instead she picked up a book on growing roses she'd found and put aside, and took it to the porch with a third cup of coffee. The old lady had loved roses. There were many in the garden, blooming luxuriantly. She leafed through the book, reading the comments written in the margins in an old-fashioned, spidery handwriting.

Halfway through the book she found a snapshot between the pages.

She stared at the picture, her heart contracting, her throat closing. Her hand shook so badly, it was difficult to focus.

It was a picture of Clint with a baby girl on his lap and a smiling woman by his side, her cheek resting against his shoulder.

They were sitting on the garden bench framed by masses of red roses.

CHAPTER SIX

LIVIA stared at the photo, transfixed, her mind a whirlpool of emotions. And questions, so many questions. Who were they, the woman and the child?

He had never mentioned a wife, nor a baby. They looked so happy, all of them. Clint, smiling, his muscled brown arm holding the baby in a protective embrace against his broad chest. The woman, blonde, blue-eyed and so obviously in love. Her hair was long and shiny and fell in soft waves around her face and over her shoulders. She wore a sky-blue shirt and white shorts, revealing long, shapely legs. She leaned into Clint with loving intimacy. They belonged together.

His wife, his baby daughter. Strange, painful emotions twisted in her chest. Her throat closed. Where were they now? What had happened?

Should she give him the photo or throw it out and pretend she'd never found it? No, she could not do that. She could not tear up and discard a picture displaying love and joy, a picture that wasn't hers.

She was in her office doing paperwork when he came through the front door at seven-thirty that night. He was dressed in a suit and tie, looking disturbingly attractive with his dark, rugged looks above the civilised clothes.

'Hi,' she said, her throat dry. She felt awkward and uncertain because of what had happened last night, because of the photo that lay on her desk in full view.

It took no time at all before his gaze settled on the picture. She watched him, her heart going wild. He grew very still. He stared at the photo, a mixture of emotions passing across his face, then the mask appeared. Aloof, remote. He did not reach for the picture. He did not say anything. He just stood there looking at it.

Her heart was racing. 'Is this your wife? Your daughter?' she asked softly. 'You never told me you had a family.'

'I don't.' The short reply was cold and hard. He pushed the jacket back and put his hands in his pockets. 'Where did you find it?' He did not look at her. There was a terrible stillness in his features.

'In a book. A book on growing roses. It was in the house and I kept it, the book, thinking there——' She stopped herself, closing her eyes for a moment. 'You didn't tell me about them,' she said tonelessly.

'No.' He turned his back on her and made for the door.

'Clint!' Despair rushed through her, making her reckless. 'Does this have anything to do with your not wanting . . . permanence with . . . with me?'

He turned to look at her, his face carved out of stone. 'Do me a favour and don't play psychoanalyst,' he said coolly. 'It's all in the past. This has nothing to do with the present.'

'Clint, you can't——'

'Let it be, Livia.' His eyes glinted dangerously. 'This is not your business and I do not intend to discuss it.' He strode out of the door.

She felt as if he had slapped her. She stared at the snapshot, seeing nothing but a blur of red roses.

For a while they'd been so happy.

Everything had been fine as long as she hadn't touched his private life. As long as she had not asked personal questions. As long as she had not asked for commitments. As long as she had not tried to reach the deepest part of him. He'd wanted to keep her at a distance, couldn't bear to have her too close. There was a line she was not allowed to cross. 'No TRESPASSING', said the sign, in huge neon letters.

What secrets lay hidden behind that aloof face, those dark eyes? He would not let her touch him. Keep away, his eyes said. Keep away, his face said. Keep away. Don't come to Kalimantan. Stay away. Leave me alone.

She stood up, her legs wooden, and went to the window. Her eyes were blinded by tears and the trees and fields and mountains were nothing but a blur in the amber light of dusk.

She wasn't sure how long she stood there, but eventually she went to the kitchen, finding Clint sitting at the table with a drink in his hand. There was a bottle of Scotch on the table. His jacket hung over a chair and he'd loosened his tie.

He did not look up when she came in, but kept staring sombrely into the amber liquid in his glass. She felt a shiver of fear run down her spine, a sense of foreboding.

He glanced up, meeting her gaze, and she didn't like the flat, dead look in his eyes.

She opened the refrigerator, fished out a can of Coke and took it upstairs with her. She sat on top of her sleeping-bag and turned on the small TV on the chest of drawers. She wanted something funny to watch.

But she couldn't laugh. She kept seeing that look in Clint's eyes. She wondered what terrors haunted him, if it had anything to do with keeping her away.

'I didn't know you had a family,' she'd asked.

'I don't,' he'd answered.

Maybe they had died tragically. Maybe he'd lost both his wife and child in a terrible accident—a car wreck, a fire. Maybe they'd fallen victim to an exotic virus.

Oh, God.

So much she did not know about him. So much he had not told her. What else was there she did not know? She closed her eyes as if it could shut out his face, but it was no use. She slipped off the bed and tiptoed back down the stairs. Why was she tiptoeing? She didn't know. He was still in the same place, sitting in the gathering darkness.

'Clint?'

He turned his face towards her, but he did not answer. She stood behind his chair and put her arms around him. It seemed the natural thing to do and the gesture was instinctive. She said nothing—she knew no words that might be any good. All she wanted was to chase the demons out of his eyes.

He did not push her away. He sat perfectly still while she went on holding him, her cheek against his hair. An eternity later he broke the embrace, took her arm and swung her around to sit on his knees. He bent his head and his mouth came down on hers with fierce, desperate passion. His arms clamped around her as if he was afraid she'd bolt away. There was nothing gentle about his kiss, nothing soft and sensuous. It was raw and hungry, and a firestorm of need broke loose inside her, mirroring the consuming heat of his kiss.

Chasing demons, came the sudden thought. A soft moan escaped her and his grip relaxed slightly. The next moment he was carrying her out of the kitchen and up the stairs. He lowered her on to his bed and began to yank off his tie and shirt. She closed her eyes, trembling with the onslaught of emotion, feeling hot tears spill over.

Moments later he was with her on the bed, kissing her again as he deftly took off her clothes until his mouth stilled on her cheek.

'You're crying,' he said roughly. 'Oh, God, Livia, I'm sorry, I'm sorry. . .'

'It's all right,' she said huskily. 'It's all right.'

'No,' he said fiercely, 'it's not all right. I'm a selfish swine.'

She put her arms around him, holding him tight. 'Don't go,' she whispered. 'Please, don't go.' She was crying silently and she didn't know why. 'Make love to me, please.'

He groaned, his mouth coming down on hers again. 'I want you,' he muttered against her lips. 'Oh, God, Livia, this is madness.'

'No, no,' she whispered. 'I need you.'

He groaned and kissed her feverishly, his mouth hot. She was aflame with need, a deep and frantic longing to be held by him, loved by him. She held him close, kissed him back with all the passion of her own feelings.

It was a feverish, frantic lovemaking and they fell asleep holding each other.

When she awoke, her face was wet with tears and Clint was gone.

*　　*　　*

She was not going to be depressed. She was determined not to give in to her feelings of unhappiness. Their passionate lovemaking had changed nothing—only the tension grew worse. Yet, she could not show him her despair. After all, she'd gone into this with her eyes open.

She had to act like a mature woman, a grown-up. He had not deceived her. She had no right to go to pieces.

She wasn't going to.

At least not while he was around.

So she was cheerful and happy. At least on the outside. But he didn't touch her any more and the day of his departure kept creeping closer and closer.

They had not forgotten her birthday. Of course they hadn't. The whole gang appeared at her door on Sunday morning at nine o'clock, all four of her brothers, her two sisters-in-law and her three nieces and nephews. They brought balloons, song and cheer, and a mountain of presents. They hugged her, kissed her, shook hands with Clint and sang happy birthday, after which they all trooped through the house and ooh-ed and ah-ed over the magic she had performed on the house. They all had suggestions and comments, and they criticised each other and laughed and joked and secretly evaluated Clint. After that the women took charge and started decorating the porch with streamers and balloons, and unpacked several boxes of goodies and a huge birthday cake.

And then the phone rang and her mother was on the line, all the way from Sweden. So she chatted and then her father chatted and then the grandchildren had to talk to Grandma and Grandpa as well, and it made for a very long and expensive phone call across the Atlantic, but that was the way it always was on birthdays.

Livia felt her spirits lift. It was exactly what she needed. Joy and cheer and people around her who loved her. How could she possibly be depressed? How lucky she was! She had a loving family, wonderful friends, a great old house to fix up. What more could she possibly want?

Wrong question. She knew what she wanted, and it was Clint, who was at that very moment engaged in a serious conversation with her four-year-old niece about the reason why squirrels had big and fluffy tails.

Tomorrow morning he was leaving. The very thought seemed to squeeze the air out of her lungs.

But this was not the day to dwell on her miseries. Today was for partying.

A while later more cars drove up, containing a dozen of her friends, all eager to help celebrate and take part in the festivities. Barbecues were lit. Huge steaks were cooked. Her brother Mac took out his guitar and sang ribald French ballads.

It was a wonderful party. The sun shone, the birds sang, the air was fragrant with summer scents and the birthday was delicious.

By eight o'clock everything had been cleaned up and people were piling into the cars and drove off.

Suddenly it was awfully quiet in the house. She could hear herself breathe. She could hear herself think.

Tomorrow morning Clint was leaving.

She walked out into the garden, veiled in the shadows of dusk, and listened to the chirps and flutterings of birds settling in for the night and a sudden desolation washed over her. She felt more alone than she'd ever felt before in her life. She was twenty-nine years old today and the man she loved was leaving tomorrow.

Footsteps came across the lawn.

'You've got quite a family,' said Clint, coming to stand next to her.

'Yes. The best.'

'They're big on celebrating, I understand.' There was a smile in his voice.

'We've always been. We moved so often, it was important to be close. Often we didn't have friends and other family around when we were in a new place. But we always had each other.' She looked at him in the failing light. 'No matter what, we always had each other.'

The silence thundered around them. He stood very still, his eyes in hers. Please, she begged silently, please let me be part of your life. She reached out a hand, instinctively, and he took it. He drew her slowly to him and held her. Then he kissed her hard and desperately and an aching need flooded her. She clung to him, feeling tears well up in her eyes. Then he abruptly thrust her from him. 'I've got to pack,' he said hoarsely. He turned on his heel and strode back into the house.

His duffel bag stood by the door. Livia stared at it, fighting for composure. He was a light traveller. He'd be gone for two years and all he had was one bag of things. His suits and other business clothes were hanging upstairs in a cupboard. She'd agreed that he could leave them there.

He wore lightweight trousers, a striped, open-necked shirt and a blazer, and he was ready to leave. It was six in the morning and the birds chirped in joyful abandon, oblivious of her misery.

'I'll call you whenever I'm near a phone to check about the house,' he said. He'd said it before. He'd given her the name and number of his lawyer who had a power of attorney. The lawyer would buy the house for him once Livia told him it was ready to be sold.

Then she would move out and a woman by the name of Suzanna Stern would move in. Suzanna Stern was a colleague, he said. She taught economics at the university and she would rent the house from him until he returned to take possession himself.

It was all very well organised.

She wished she had never bought the house. She wished she had never met Clint Bracamonte. She wished . . .

'Goodbye, Livia.' His voice was rough and he took her in his arms and kissed her hard. Then he let her go, picked up the bag and stalked out of the house towards the car.

As if in a trance, she watched him as he opened the door, got in, closed the door. His face appeared in profile behind the window.

He started the engine and the sound roared in her ears. The car drove off.

He did not look back. He did not even wave.

She scraped and sanded and painted and cried. She installed a new back door, replaced a cracked pane of glass in one of the windows and kept on crying. She laid Mexican tiles in the sun-room and wept. She rented a sander and sanded all the wooden floors, dripping tears on the raw wood, making dark stains. Every muscle in her body ached. Her heart hurt. She couldn't stop crying. She was a mess.

All she could think of was Clint. Clint making love to her. Clint with a tiny bird in his big hands. Clint with a baby girl on his lap.

She loved him. She wanted him. She hated him for doing what he was doing to her.

She should paint the walls purple. She should put jungle-flower wallpaper in the bathrooms. She should plant poison ivy in the garden. She should...

Three weeks went by and it didn't get any easier. She was never, ever going to forget him. She would never love another man. She would shrivel away with misery.

One day a dusty pick-up truck that had seen better days drove up the drive. It had Pennsylvania licence plates. A woman emerged, then a small girl dragging a battered suitcase. They came up to the front porch.

The woman wore a wrinkled skirt and blouse and she looked tired. She had dark circles under her eyes and her dull brown hair hung limp around her face. She wore no make-up and she looked pale and faded. Livia opened the front door. A blast of July heat assaulted her.

'Is Mr Bracamonte at home?' the woman asked without introducing herself.

Livia shook her head. 'No. He doesn't live here right now. He's abroad.'

The little girl looked bedraggled, her grey eyes huge in a small pinched face. Her shorts looked worn and there was a large stain on the front of her T-shirt. 'Is he still in the jungle?' she asked, disappointment alive on her freckled face.

'Yes, he is.' Livia stared at the girl, gripped by a terrible apprehension. She dragged in air and looked back at the woman. 'I'm Olivia Jordan,' she said. 'I'm remodelling the house. Is there something I can do for you?'

'I'm Janet, and this is Tammy. I'm bringing her here because it's time for her father to face up to his responsibilities and take care of her now.' There was ill-concealed censure in the woman's voice.

Livia froze. It was as if the ground gave way under her feet. She stared at the woman, then back at Tammy, and the photo flashed before her eyes. The baby had been small. It was hard to tell if she was the same child as the girl standing in front of her. She searched the woman's face, but there was no resemblance at all to the blonde beauty on the photograph.

'My mother died,' said Tammy. 'And now I'm going to live with my father. I'm going to live in the jungle.' It was said matter-of-factly. It was not the voice of a small child. It sounded old and wise and touched Livia to the core.

'There's no one else to take her,' the woman went on.

'Can I have a glass of water, please?' the girl asked. 'I'm very thirsty.'

Livia tucked a strand of hair behind her ear. 'Yes, yes, of course. Why don't you come in?' She led them to the cool kitchen, poured lemonade in a daze, moving automatically, her thoughts tumbling through her head, tossed around by a storm of emotions.

'I can't stay,' the woman said nervously, sitting on the edge of the chair. She looked as if she wanted to bolt out. 'I've got to get back home. I gotta go to work tomorrow.'

'To Pennsylvania?' Livia asked, remembering the licence plates on the pick-up. 'Is that where you're from?'

'Yes.' The woman gulped the drink.

'We drove all day,' Tammy said. 'I've never been in a car that long. I didn't know it was that far.'

Livia lowered herself into a chair. 'Please tell me what is going on here. Mr Bracamonte is out of the country and it's difficult to contact him.'

'I can't keep her,' the woman said again, a desperate note to her voice. 'It's his turn now.'

'And you're not Tammy's mother?'

'Her mother's dead,' came the succinct reply. 'I tried to help, but there wasn't nothing I could do. I'm just a neighbour and I don't know there's any other family. Janine never mentioned there was any.'

Livia glanced at the little girl, her heart breaking. Tammy sat slumped in her chair, looking exhausted and defeated. She'd been in a car all day, to be delivered to a strange place like an unwanted parcel. Mother dead. No family. No one who wanted her. And now her father wasn't here, either.

Livia thought of her own many moves to strange places, new houses, new countries, new schools. She had never been alone, passed around like an unwanted package. She'd been with her parents and brothers, feeling safe, despite all the strangeness. Safe because there was love in her life, because she belonged.

She smiled at the girl. 'You look hungry. Would you like something to eat? I can make some peanut butter sandwiches.'

The woman came to her feet. 'I gotta go.' She pushed her hair away from her face in a nervous gesture. 'Just tell her father he's got to take care of her now.' She bent over and kissed Tammy on the cheek. 'Be brave, honey. Everything's gonna be all right.' Then she turned and without saying anything else she rushed into the entry-way, back to the front door. Livia followed her, watching in stunned disbelief as the woman got back into the pick-up and drove off.

Slowly she went back to the porch. The girl sat stiffly upright in her chair, her legs dangling. There were small scabs around her ankles, mosquito bites scratched open.

She looked up, her grey eyes meeting Livia's. Her face looked old and wise for such a small girl. Her hands lay clasped together in her lap.

'Will you help me find my father?' she asked solemnly.

Livia's heart contracted. She did the only thing she could. She smiled at Tammy. 'Of course I'll help you find your father.'

Tammy wolfed down a peanut butter sandwich, a glass of milk and a bunch of green grapes. She'd said very little.

'Is this my father's house?' she asked when she was finished.

Livia nodded. 'Yes.' It was easier this way.

'It's very big.'

'Yes, it is.'

'I live in a trailer. Well, not any more. It was old and very small. When it rained, it leaked. And there was no yard. Just dirt. This is a very big yard.'

Livia nodded.

'My mother said my father was rich. He must be if he has a house like this.' She picked up her glass and drank the last few drops of milk that had settled on the bottom.

'Would you like some more milk?' Livia asked, wondering desperately what she was going to do with this child.

'Yes, please.'

She poured more milk, aware of a terrible anger gathering inside her. She wished she could pick up the phone and call Clint, give him a piece of her mind. How dared he go off to the end of the world while he had a little daughter living in a dilapidated trailer?

She saw in her mind the picture of Clint, the baby on his knees, the smiling woman by his side.

Something was wrong. Terribly wrong.

'Sara? I need help.' Livia tried to relax her hand gripping the phone receiver. 'You won't believe what happened,' she began.

The house was silent. Tammy was asleep in Clint's bedroom, wearing one of Livia's cotton T-shirts and clutching a ragged teddy bear. Even asleep her face looked old and worried.

Having finished her second glass of milk, Tammy had automatically cleared the table and started washing the dishes. 'I know how,' she'd said when Livia told her she didn't need to. 'I always wash the dishes.'

'We have a dishwasher,' Livia had pointed out. 'I'll show you how it works.'

The kitchen work done, Tammy had politely asked where she should sleep, and then had taken her shabby bag to the room and unpacked. The bed had been stripped and the sheets washed, and she'd told Livia she could make the bed herself. She always made her own bed.

Livia needed to talk to somebody, so she'd called Sara.

'What happened?' asked Sara patiently.

Livia took a deep breath and told her.

'Clint has a *daughter*?' Sara's voice was high with astonishment. 'How old is she?'

'She says she's six. Oh, Sara, she's such a scruffy little waif! She's too skinny and her clothes are all rags and she looks so *old*. And this woman, a neighbour, just dumped her here.'

'What about the mother?'

'She's dead. You should have heard Tammy say it. She announced it so matter-of-factly it made my skin crawl.'

'What do you think happened?'

'I have no idea. I don't know anything and I'm afraid to ask. She lived in a trailer, though. She volunteered the information after she informed me that this place is a very nice house. She was very businesslike about it.'

'I'll come over first thing in the morning,' said Sara. 'I'll bring some of Mandy's clothes.'

After she'd hung up, Livia sat in her office staring at the wall.

Clint's daughter. A scruffy little girl living in a trailer with rags for clothes. She thought of the picture of Clint, his wife, and the baby on his lap. They hadn't died, as she had thought. The marriage must have broken up.

'It's all in the past,' he'd said. 'This has nothing to do with the present.'

For hours now she'd tried not to think about it, not to let the anger rise to the surface. It was rising now.

How could he have abandoned his own child? How could he have allowed his own child to live in poverty? How could she have been so mistaken about him? She, who thought she knew men, who could gauge honesty, integrity, honour?

How could she have been so wrong?

So many questions. So many long, sleepless hours while the dark night stretched on, offering no answers.

Sara arrived at ten the next morning. Tammy had awoken an hour earlier. She had made her own bed. After breakfast she'd stacked the dishes in the dishwasher, wiped the counter and table and then started sweeping the porch. The broom looked too big in her small hands. Livia let her go, watching her, her throat aching. She was relieved when Sara drove up the drive. She put on water for coffee.

Sara brought a box full of clothes and a bag of fresh doughnuts for fortification. They left the clothes in the hall and proceeded to the porch for coffee. Tammy had finished her sweeping. Livia introduced the two.

Tammy looked solemn. 'Is there anything else I can do?' she asked politely.

'Yes,' said Livia. 'You can sit down with us and have a doughnut and some juice. How about apple juice?'

'Oh, yes, please. I can get it myself.'

'You sit,' said Livia. 'I'll bring it all out together.'

So they sat and talked while they had drinks and doughnuts.

'You've been working hard,' said Livia to Tammy.

'Oh, I always clean and sweep,' said Tammy, wiping powdered sugar from her mouth. 'I had to help my mother. She wasn't . . . I mean she . . .' She sighed and lowered her gaze to her hands. 'She was sick.'

Livia ached for her. 'I'm sorry, Tammy,' she said gently. 'You must have gone through a difficult time.' What else could she say? She hated feeling so helpless.

Tammy looked up again. 'She's in heaven now.' Her voice was calm. 'I cry a lot, but I know now she's happy. So really, I shouldn't feel sad, should I?'

Livia glanced at Sara, her throat constricted.

Sara glanced over at Tammy. 'It's all right to feel sad, Tammy. It's all right to cry.'

Tammy took a drink from her juice, both hands around the glass. Her hands were trembling. 'I wish my dad was here,' she said in a small voice.

'He didn't know you were coming,' Livia said. She didn't know that as a fact, of course, but she was pretty sure. 'When did you see him last?'

Tammy's eyes widened. 'Oh, I don't know. I was little.' She slipped off the chair. 'I have a picture. I'll show you.' She rushed inside.

Livia looked at Sara. 'He didn't even go to see her when he was here for two months,' she said tonelessly. 'How can this be?'

Tammy was back almost instantly, a photo in her hand. Livia's throat went dry when she looked at the tattered, much handled snapshot. It showed a tiny Tammy, trying to walk solo, and Clint hunkered down, arms wide, ready to catch her.

'That's my dad,' said Tammy proudly. 'My mother said he's a very important man, very smart. He's a scientist and he lives in the jungle doing very important work. It's on the other side of the world and that's why he can't come and see us. Maybe when he's finished he'll come back. Do you think he'll come back soon?'

Livia swallowed. 'I don't know, Tammy, but I'm going to find out, OK?'

What was she saying? She was making a promise. She was getting herself involved in other people's lives, in a situation that was none of her business.

But yesterday when that weary-looking woman had dropped off this little waif at her door it had become her business.

'Listen,' she said. 'I wonder if you'd get us some blackberries for lunch. There's a whole row of bushes at the end of the yard, and they have no thorns.'

Tammy's eyes grew wide with wonder. 'I can pick them?' she asked. 'Really?'

Livia smiled. 'Only the ripe ones, and you can eat some while you're picking.'

Having found a bowl, Tammy took off down the garden path. Her legs looked thin and fragile. There was a hole in the toe of her canvas trainer. Sara and Livia watched her go.

'Oh, my God,' whispered Sara, 'that poor thing.'

'I don't understand,' Livia said tightly, trying to keep control over her anger. 'How could he allow this to happen?'

Sara bit her lip. 'It happens all the time, Liv,' she said gently. 'Lots of fathers don't pay child support after a divorce.'

She shook her head numbly. 'But that's not like Clint, Sara. He's got integrity and principles. It's not at all what he would do!'

'What else could it be, then?'

'I don't know.' She sighed wearily. 'What do I do now?'

'You'll have to tell Clint;' said Sara.

'How? It took almost two months before he got the news of his grandmother's death.'

'So sending a telegram won't do any good?'

'No.' She pressed her hands against her eyes. 'Maybe he doesn't want her. If he had wanted her, would she look like she does? He *abandoned* her!'

'It's all in the past. This has nothing to do with the present . . .' The words echoed in her head. Well, the past had come back to haunt the present.

They had more coffee. They discussed the situation, analysed, hypothesised, speculated, deliberated and calculated.

There was, of course, only one solution, and so in the end they had to put it into words and make plans.

Tammy would stay with Sara and Jack and their two girls, and Livia would get on a series of planes, go to the deep dark Kalimantan jungle and find Clint.

There was nothing but endless green rainforest below her, with the river snaking through it like a shiny ribbon. Somewhere beneath that canopy of green, further into the interior, was the longhouse village where Clint lived and worked—several more days of travel from the trading post where the tiny missionary supply plane would drop her in the next few minutes.

She was prepared for the trip, at least she hoped she was. It was a good thing she'd been so curious about Clint's life here; she'd gleaned quite a bit of information from the stories he had told her. From home she'd brought her backpack, flashlight, Swiss army knife and cotton sheet and a light blanket. In the mountainous regions of the interior, the nights cooled down considerably. In the small logging town where she'd flown from Balikpapan, she'd purchased a sleeping mat, a mosquito net, a couple of sarongs and a blue enamelled mug and plate. She had bug repellent and anti-itch cream and a few other necessities. In spite of the unsavoury nature of her mission, she could not help but be excited about her trek into the rainforest.

After she landed at the trading post, she would ask the village headman for advice. She would need to rent a boat and a couple of guides and porters to help her find her way to Clint's village.

The plane landed on a grass landing strip, bumping precariously across the rough surface. Dark-eyed, curious children were everywhere, watching as the supplies were taken off and loaded on to a cart drawn by a water buffalo. A teenage boy wearing blue satin jogging shorts and a Coca Cola T-shirt took her backpack. 'I will take you to the headman,' he said.

Accompanied by a swarm of curious children, she followed him to the longhouse and she peered at it in fascination as the stilted structure appeared in front of her.

Her first longhouse! She had seen pictures of them, of course, but she had never actually seen one of the huge thatch-roofed structures built off the ground to protect its inhabitants from enemies, animals and the forest floor's voracious insects and micro-organisms. She climbed the notched pole to the huge communal veranda that stretched the entire length of the building and the boy led her to the headman's quarters, only to find he was not there. The place seemed almost deserted, which was no surprise. Either the people were out working their garden plots, or they were at the landing strip.

'Please wait here,' he said in Indonesian, pointing to a straight chair outside the room and putting down her pack.

'*Terimah kasih*,' she said, and smiled. 'I'll wait.' So did the children. They parked themselves opposite her and stared and giggled.

A barefoot young girl wearing a crisp pink blouse and a batik sarong glided up to her with a glass of hot tea, giving her a welcoming smile. She was graceful and beautiful, her smooth skin glowing, her large eyes dark and curious.

She was the headman's daughter, she explained, and he would be home soon. Livia took a sip of the hot tea. It was sweet and faintly spicy. Laughter and commotion erupted at one end of the veranda and another group of boisterous children came rushing along the creaking plank floor, laughing and tripping over each other. The girl's smile widened. '*Pak Clint ada!*' she said.

It took a moment to register what the girl had said. Livia froze. Her heart gave a sickening lurch as she noticed the tall figure amid the group of children, the obvious instigator of their enjoyment.

She forgot to breathe. She had not expected this. Her mind was not ready for it. Clint was not supposed to be here. He was supposed to be three days' travel up river in a tiny forest village.

He wore khaki shorts and a blue T-shirt. His legs and arms were dark and the muscles rippled with energy as he strode along the veranda in her direction. She took in a desperate gulp of warm, moist air. This was not what she wanted to feel, this instant, sweet longing. She could not keep her eyes off him. His hair was longish, his face alive with a teasing grin. His arm shot out, grabbed one of the little boys and tucked the kid under his arm and held him tight around his middle. The boy squirmed and flailed his arms and legs. The kids squealed in delight.

Then Clint saw her. He stopped dead in his tracks and the grin vanished from his face. He released his grip on the boy and the kid slipped to the wooden floor.

Her heart pounded painfully against her ribs and she realised she was trembling all over. The children that had been watching her ran over and joined the others, clustering around Clint. He looked down on them, saying something she could not hear. Laughing, they all ran off.

Livia watched as Clint strode towards her, stopped, loomed over her. The girl smiled up at him. 'I'll bring you tea,' she said, and slipped into the headman's quarters.

There was an eerie silence as they stared at each other. His chin and cheeks were dark with the beginnings of a beard. His eyes were black as coal.

'My God,' he said, his voice low and incredulous. 'What the hell are you doing here?'

CHAPTER SEVEN

LIVIA stared up at him, the shock of seeing him so unexpectedly momentarily rendering her speechless. There it was again—the need, the yearning. Instantly, inevitably. She hated herself for it. She didn't want a man who was so careless with his love. A man who had abandoned his own child. A man who loved and then left.

She didn't like sitting down while he was hovering over her, so she came shakily to her feet. 'I'm on the way to your village. I . . . need to talk to you. I didn't expect to see you here.'

'I'm picking up supplies.' Clint's face was taut. 'Dammit, Livia! You *know* I didn't want you to come here!' he said furiously.

She certainly did. He had made it abundantly clear before, and apparently he hadn't changed his mind. Obviously he had not been pining away for her and he didn't care to see her now. Well, she hadn't come here for her own purposes. She felt suddenly deflated and empty. She said nothing.

His eyes bored into hers. 'Livia, this wasn't in the plan,' he went on, his voice rough. 'I thought you understood.'

She gave him a stony stare. 'I did, perfectly,' she said coldly, crossing her arms in front of her chest. 'You wanted a nice, clean, temporary affair. I was available, willing, and stupid enough to fall for it and——'

'You're getting right back on that plane,' he interrupted her harshly. He leaned over and picked up her backpack.

She dropped herself back down on the chair. 'I am not getting back on that plane!' She gave him a shrivelling look. 'Rest assured, I didn't come here to tell you I can't live without you, because I can. I'm very good at it, actually.' She had her pride. Besides, after what had happened she wouldn't want him if he were presented to her on a silver platter.

His mouth curved sceptically, fanning her anger.

'You've got quite an ego, haven't you?' she said on a low note. 'Does it occur to you I might have a reason for coming here that has nothing to do with my supposed insatiable passion for you?'

He lifted a mocking brow. 'Your lust for travel, perhaps? I thought you were going to wait till the house was finished.'

'So I was, but I changed my mind. There's something we——'

The deafening roar of an aeroplane low overhead broke into her words. Clint cursed under his breath and dropped the backpack on the veranda floor. 'You know what that means?' he asked.

Oh, yes, she did. 'It means the plane has left and I'm not on it. And it won't be back for two weeks and I'm stuck in the rainforest in a longhouse without western-style plumbing and I may have to eat bee-larvae soup.' Oh, God, she hoped not. That really might test her capacity for enjoying things adventurous.

He stroked his chin which made a rasping sound over the dark stubble. 'In terms of that at least, you seem to have some grasp on reality.'

A grasp on reality. She hated him for his smug arrogance. What did he know about reality sitting here in the rainforest thousands of miles away from a child who yearned to be with him? A child who hadn't seen him since she was a baby and who'd made him into some sort of a god, a fantasy father created in her mind because the real one was not around.

Poor Tammy. Anxiety churned inside her. Was she doing the right thing? What was Clint going to do with a six-year-old daughter? The same questions and worries had plagued her ever since she'd made the decision to go to Borneo. It certainly had taken the fun and adventure out of a trip that should be an experience of a lifetime. Here she was in the Borneo jungle in an old traditional longhouse, whose older occupants most certainly had been headhunters in their younger years, and she was having an argument with Clint instead of enjoying her surroundings.

A commotion at the end of the veranda distracted their attention.

'Here comes the headman,' said Clint. 'We're visitors here and he'll ask you to be his guest if he likes you. Otherwise you're in trouble. No motels around here.'

She smiled sweetly. 'Well, then, I'll just have to make him like me, won't I?'

Several people approached, the women wearing sarongs and blouses, the men shorts and T-shirts. They looked as if they'd spent their day working in the fields, which probably was the case.

The headman's name was Pak Ubang. He was a short, muscled man with tattoos running up and down his arms. He shook her hand and wished her *selamat datang*, and was delighted with her gift of T-shirts depicting various scenic American landmarks.

The headman's daughter arrived with more tea.

'You travel alone?' Pak Ubang asked Livia in Indonesian, his shrewd eyes observing her keenly.

'Yes, I do,' she said truthfully.

'I have never seen a woman like you travel this far alone.'

She smiled demurely. 'I have heard many good things about the people and the forest and I wanted to see for myself.' It was true enough, although it was not the real reason that she had come. It annoyed her to be so aware of Clint sitting there listening in on this conversation, waves of displeasure radiating from him.

'You speak Indonesian very well,' said the headman.

'As a child I lived on Java with my parents, and also in Malaysia.' Indonesian was a local variant of Malay. 'Children learn quickly.'

Pak Ubang nodded in agreement. 'Will you write about us and take photographs?' he enquired.

'I would like to take photographs if I may, but I am not a writer. I am a traveller because I like to see how other people live and to learn from them.'

He seemed to find this amusing. 'Pak Clint is studying the people in his village—the things they grow, the animals they hunt and the things they find in the forest. Now you are here. What would you like to learn from us?'

She smiled. 'Joy, happiness.'

He raised his brows. 'You do not have joy and happiness?'

She grinned at him. 'I want more. We can never have enough, can we?'

He laughed out loud, as did the other people who'd been listening and watching.

'You will be my guest tonight,' said Pak Ubang, 'and we will show you joy and happiness. We will eat, drink and dance. Do you like to eat, drink and dance?'

'Yes,' said Livia.

Clint had not said a word, but she could feel his eyes burning on her through the whole exchange. She wondered what he was thinking. She'd had no choice but to say what she had. She couldn't very well have told the truth about the much admired Pak Clint—that he had a little daughter in America and he'd abandoned her. It was not the sort of thing that would be either understood or respected in a traditional community such as this where children were loved and cherished.

The longhouse veranda was beginning to fill up as people gathered around to have a look at her and wish her welcome. Then everybody took off to the river for their evening baths and Pak Ubang's daughter took Livia under her wing, including her in a group of several women and children.

She hadn't had a shower for what seemed like ages, and it was a delight to feel water on her skin again, even though she was covered up with a sarong for modesty's sake. Washing with that wet thing clinging to her was not easy. Drying off and putting on a T-shirt and a dry sarong was not easy either with all the kids' eyes on her to see how she would manage this feat without showing any nudity. As she struggled clumsily, she suppressed the temptation to drop the damned wet sarong and give them what they wanted.

She should consider it an educational experience: See, I look just like everybody else—just a little taller and a little paler.

Back at the longhouse, food was served in Pak Ubang's family quarters, served by his wife, who had a shy smile and long extended earlobes weighed down with heavy brass rings. Sitting on rattan mats spread on the plank floor, they ate steamed hill rice and chunks of wild boar just off the fire—all perfectly tasty. She was aware of Clint watching her, his eyes dark and inscrutable. She tried to ignore him, but it was impossible. Clint wasn't a man you could ignore. His presence seemed to affect the very air she breathed. With every breath she took in she felt her anger growing.

After dinner there were more drinks and more stories and lots of laughter and then the dancing began. Two string instruments played by young men supplied the music. Young girls, lovely and graceful in their colourful traditional dress, fluttered delicately in imitations of birds in flight.

After this things got a bit wilder. Barefoot men dressed in leopardskins, decorated shields and beaded headdresses with huge feathers performed a war dance, waving dangerous-looking knives.

'They're called *mandau*,' Clint whispered in her ear. 'They used to use them for headhunting. The Dayaks were great headhunters.'

'I've heard.' She'd seen pictures and old photographs. It was something from the past, if not from too distant a past. She glanced over at several old men, their bodies covered with tattoos. They were laughing and having a good time. 'I suppose those grandpas over there could tell us stories,' she whispered.

'They're not too happy being reminded, so it's better not mentioned.'

She wouldn't have dreamed of it.

It was magic—the music, the colours, the movements, the whole atmosphere in the longhouse. She was enthralled. The *arak* helped considerably to lighten her mood; the potent local spirits had her happy and light-headed after one glass.

Everybody seemed to be having a good time. She sipped more *arak*. Exhaustion was beginning to overwhelm her. Possibly culture shock as well. Only a few days ago she had sat in a brand-new state-of-the-art air-conditioned American kitchen plotting this trip, and now she was here sitting on an ancient wooden floor in the jungle watching men jump around in leopardskins.

The next morning she awakened in a small room full of women and children. She was lying on her mat on the floor, covered by the sheet and blanket she had brought. Someone had rigged up her mosquito net, although no one else used one. There were only vague memories about how she had ended up in this room late at night. Clint supporting her, unrolling her sleeping mat, covering her up. Outside on the veranda everybody still had been partying.

Around her everybody was blissfully asleep on their mats. She felt stiff and sore. The plank floor was hard and she'd slept without a pillow. She was still wearing the T-shirt and batik sarong she'd put on after her river bath the night before.

The window shutter was open and she listened to the noises coming from the jungle outside—birds, insects, high-pitched screeches she could not identify.

Beyond the walls of the room, she heard human noises—people moving around, talking.

She could no longer stay down. She needed to stretch. Sitting up, she rummaged through her bag and found a brush and pulled it through her hair with a few quick strokes. Carefully she came to her feet and retied her sarong. Trying not to disturb the other sleepers, she tiptoed to the door. The floor creaked. The door squeaked. No one awakened. She stepped on to the longhouse veranda into the chilly morning air. A thick veil of mist hung between the trees and she shivered. She glanced left and right, seeing all the many doors, wondering behind which one Clint was sleeping.

It had been in the room right next to hers. The door opened minutes after she'd stepped on to the veranda and several people emerged, Clint among them.

'*Selamat pagi*,' they said, almost in unison.

She smiled. '*Selamat pagi*,' she returned.

Clint gave her a searching look. 'How are you?' he asked quietly in English.

'I'm fine.'

'I have aspirin if you need it.'

She didn't need it and she had some herself if she did.

'I don't have a hangover,' she said tightly. 'I've never had a hangover in my life.' The stubble on his chin had grown some more. He was getting that devilish look again. The clean-shaven man in suit and tie was hard to call to mind.

'*Arak* is potent stuff.'

'I noticed. I didn't have that much. I was exhausted last night, that's all. It was all quite overwhelming. It was quite a party.'

'I hope it gave you joy and happiness,' he said drily.

'Oh, it did,' she said lightly. 'I love this stuff. That's why I like to travel.'

He nodded. 'To see how other people live and to learn from them.'

'Oh, shut up,' she said irritably.

A faint smile curved his mouth. 'You were very good, you know. So sincere, so serene. I almost believed you.'

But not quite. He believed she'd come here to be with him. A strange whoop-whoop-whooping came from the forest.

'What's that?' she asked.

'Gibbon monkeys.' He glanced over to where the men had made a fire. 'We'd better go and join them for tea or they'll think we're impolite.'

The air was chilly and damp and the hot sweet tea tasted good. More people joined them. Breakfast was prepared—rice with smoked deer meat, and papaya, freshly cut from a tree before her very eyes.

The veranda overlooked the river. After breakfast, Livia stood at the railing and watched two men loading a long dugout canoe with several boxes and bags. Clint appeared by her side and immediately she felt every nerve jump to attention.

'We're leaving in half an hour,' he said brusquely. 'I have no choice but to take you with me. You can't hang around here for two weeks and impose on their hospitality, waiting for the next plane to take you out of here.'

Anger washed over her. She was not his responsibility. He did not have to take charge of her. 'I had no intention of hanging around here for two weeks,' she said, trying not to let her anger show. There were too many people around, watching, probably sensing the strained atmosphere between them. Showing anger was not cool in the Orient, she knew.

'Get your things so they can load them in the boat,' he told her and turned away.

There was no choice. Half an hour later they chug-chugged up the misty river, waved off by the villagers. There were four men besides the two of them—the owner of the boat and his son, and two porters from Clint's village. The longboat had been outfitted with an outboard motor, much to her regret. The noise was annoying. How much more peaceful it would be just to paddle lazily up the jungle river and listen to the forest sounds.

How much more enjoyable it would be if she had come here on a peaceful mission.

She did not feel peaceful. Her heart felt heavy in her chest and her stomach felt as if she'd swallowed a rock. She kept stealing glances at Clint sitting in front of her, feeling her throat close in despair. He wasn't the man she'd thought he was. But deep down she still yearned for him—the fantasy man she had shared her bed with, the fantasy man she had loved.

Silent and aloof, he seemed alien again. How was it possible to feel such a gaping chasm between them when once she'd felt so close? How was it possible she had been so deceived? She forced the bitter thoughts away and concentrated on the scenery, taking in the wild rocky riverbanks and the dense green forest stretching beyond—an ancient world throbbing with unseen life. Despite everything, she could feel the excitement return—that odd restless enthusiasm for experiencing things new and unknown.

The sun grew hotter and burned off the morning mist. She slathered sunscreen all over her exposed skin. They stopped for lunch at a rocky beach at the edge of the river. The forest shade was cool and damp compared to the blazing sun on the water, and she glanced around in awe at the massive trees festooned with delicate, trailing orchids and giant, drooping ferns.

The headman's wife had prepared food for them— steamed rice, smoked deer meat, vegetables and chillies wrapped in banana-leaf packets for each of them.

The men built a fire and filled a blackened kettle with river water and tea-leaves for the inevitable tea. They ate and talked, but Livia mostly listened. Clint was calm and polite to her, but his manner was distant and his behaviour grated on her nerves. Having finished eating, she came to her feet and began walking a little way down a narrow trail. She felt restless and needed to move. Clint was immediately behind her.

'Don't take off on your own,' he said. 'It's dangerous.'

'I wasn't taking off,' she said irritably. 'I just wanted to stretch my legs. I've been sitting for hours.' She glanced over at the fire where the men were still sitting, in no apparent hurry to leave. She felt a growing need to get rid of her news, to let him know about Tammy, but there never seemed to be a good time. It wasn't something she could toss out over tea and rice.

She took a deep breath and looked Clint straight in the face. 'We need to talk,' she said. 'It's important.'

'Not now,' he said curtly. 'We'll have time when we get to the village. We've got two damned weeks to talk.' He looked at her grimly. 'But you'd better understand that there's nothing you can say to make me change my mind, Livia. You can't stay with me.'

The heat of anger rushed to her face. 'You've made that excruciatingly clear, and I have no intention of staying longer than absolutely necessary! I'll take the next plane out!'

'Good. Now, let's get going.'

Her stomach churned. She did not recognise this man. She hated him. She hated herself for having been such a fool to fall for him.

They all climbed back in the longboat, encouraged by the raucous call from a big black bird sitting on a tree limb overhanging the river. It had long white and black tail feathers. 'A hornbill,' said Clint. 'Those feathers in the warriors' headdresses you saw last night are hornbill feathers.'

The river was getting narrower and rougher with huge boulders and shallow rapids making passage difficult. The boatman pulled the motor in, afraid it would be damaged, and the men began to paddle and pole their way through the shallow water. Several times they had to get out and drag the boat across the rapids. The massive trees closed overhead, forming a green tunnel with only filtered light coming through. It was magical and primal and like nothing she had ever seen before. Here was a world unchanged for millennia, a world untouched by civilisation, following its own rhythms.

Late in the afternoon they pulled the boat up on the riverbank. To keep the sand flies away, a fire was built right away, although the humid heat of the afternoon still lingered.

Clint told her to stay put and rest and the men went off to gather saplings and leaves to build a sleeping shelter. Livia watched with fascination as the men constructed a *pondok*, a raised platform of saplings lashed together with rattan vines and covered with a sloping roof made of three layers of huge fan-shaped jungle leaves. All six of them would sleep there tonight, safe from crawling insects and other unwanted creatures that roamed the damp, leafy forest floor.

Clint worked right along with the men, moving with agility and working with obvious expertise. He was at home in this environment. Once again she thought of him wearing a suit and tie and it was hard to call up the image.

The *pondok* finished, it was time for a river bath. Livia intended to go off by herself but Clint followed her to the large group of boulders that made up a natural sort of pool. The other men simply stayed right where the boat had been pulled up on the riverbank.

'I'd like some privacy,' she said, and he shrugged impatiently.

'You might as well get used to the idea that no such thing exists here. I'm staying put to keep an eye out for you. This is not your friendly neighbourhood swimming pool. I know what to look out for and you don't.'

Well, there was no arguing that. She glanced around. 'What's to look out for?'

He shrugged. 'Snakes, insects.'

He threw off his clothes and waded naked into the water and she watched his back, her pulse quickening. She took off her own clothes, wrapped a sarong around her and followed him in.

'Are you all right?' he asked, soaping his chest.

'I'm fine,' she said. 'Just tired.' The understatement of the year. She did not want to look at his chest. It brought memories of the feel of his heart beating under her cheek, of happy nights full of loving.

It had all been wrong, wrong.

She turned her back on him and began to wash. She longed to take off the sarong, but the boatmen and porters were only a short distance away and Clint was right behind her. Once it would not have mattered for him to see her naked; it would have been an exhilarating experience being here with him on this jungle river. Now all she could think of was to get away from him and his soapy, muscled torso.

She washed quickly, waded out of the water and dried herself, putting on a clean T-shirt and a dry sarong. She spread out her towel and the wet sarong in a patch of sunlight to dry. Sitting on a rock, she brushed out her hair and hoped it would dry.

Her eye caught the brilliant blue of a kingfisher in flight, gliding from branch to branch. Hidden in the verdant greenery, other birds chirped and warbled their joyful songs.

'It's so beautiful here,' she said. 'So...untouched.'

'Yes,' he said. His eyes met hers and for a moment she saw something flicker in their dark depths. Then it was gone. He turned away and spread his towel out on a sun-heated rock.

She'd felt an impulsive need to share her observations and feelings, and for a moment she had forgotten that there was nothing now between them—nothing to share. She yanked her brush through her wet hair until it hurt.

Back by the fire, she watched the men put rice, river water and smoked deer meat into green sections of bamboo which they placed in the fire to cook. She took out her notebook and wrote until it was time to eat. She always took notes on her trips and one day she would do something with them, she was sure.

The charred sections of bamboo were split lengthwise and the hot food deposited on large green leaves. They ate with their fingers and drank copious amounts of hot black tea.

It turned dark quickly and they all sat around the fire and talked for a while, but she was too tired to follow the conversation. She came to her feet and excused herself, saying she wanted to sleep. She climbed up the *pondok* and rolled out her sleeping mat. Clint followed her up and strung up both their mosquito nets without a word. She lay down, tucked in the net and pulled her sheet and blanket over her. It was not a room at the Hilton, but it was a place to stretch out.

Clint went back to the fire and she listened to the men's voices while sleep eluded her. The air was alive with sounds of insects—a cacophony of rasping, shrieking and buzzing. Mating calls, she assumed, not lullabies for her, who did not belong in this forest.

She pretended sleep when Clint climbed up the *pondok* and lay down next to her. Her body tensed at his nearness. The other men followed and the platform creaked and swayed as they settled in to sleep. She was uncomfortably aware of Clint's body right next to hers, of the wall of emotion separating them.

She did not respect this man. She despised him for what he had done and he did not deserve her love.

So why then did she feel this aching need? Why then did she want to touch him, feel his arms around her? She lay rigidly on the sleeping mat, remembering Tammy's small face, wishing somehow the whole nightmare would be over.

'Tomorrow will be a hard day,' he said into the darkness. 'We'll have to walk.'

She hadn't fooled him; he knew she wasn't asleep. 'I'm all right,' she said, but her voice sounded strained. 'You've told me before. Leeches, sweat-bees, mud, snakes. Goodnight.'

The next morning after breakfast, the boatman and his son turned back with the longboat and the four of them set off down the forest path. The three men had divided the supplies among them and carried the huge bundles on their backs. One of the two porters headed up the line, followed by Clint. She was behind Clint and the other porter was behind her.

At times they would lose sight of the river and there was nothing but walls of green foliage and huge trees blocking out the sky. The air was warm and damp and it was difficult to breathe. It was difficult to walk. Broken branches, barbed vines and slippery, rotting leaves made the path treacherous. Having Clint walk in front of her was not as much of a distraction as she had feared. Most of the time she was looking where she was putting her feet, rather than at the back of his head or his muscled back.

And, as expected, there were leeches, disgusting slippery worm-like creatures that needed to be plucked off before they started their meal. It was a new experience for her, but not one that she would have minded doing without.

They had a mid-morning break and two porters went off to do some fishing for lunch, leaving Livia and Clint by the fire. She took out her notebook and began to write, but it was hard to concentrate with Clint only feet away.

They were alone. Her heart began a dull throbbing. She glanced at him. He was staring in the fire, absorbed in thought. She closed her notebook and put it down. She picked up her mug and took a fortifying swig of the sweet tea.

'I want to ask you something,' she began, and she saw him tense. She wiped a damp strand of hair out of her face. 'Remember the photograph I found of you and your wife and the baby?'

He looked up, his jaw a hard line. 'Yes.'

She took a deep breath. 'Were you divorced?'

He gave her a penetrating stare. 'No. What the hell is this all about?' He snapped a small, dead branch in pieces and tossed them on the fire.

No. He had said no. Her hands tightened around the mug of tea. He hadn't been divorced. Which meant he'd been married. He'd been married while he'd been staying with her in the house. He'd been married and his wife and daughter had been living in a leaky trailer. He'd lied to her. She began to tremble with an uncontrollable anger. Putting the cup on the ground, she struggled to her feet and walked away from him, her legs shaking.

He was right behind her. 'What the hell is this all about, Livia? What is the matter with you?'

She clenched her hands into fists. 'There's nothing the matter with me! The question is what is the matter with you!'

He gave a long-suffering sigh. 'Please, do enlighten me.'

He was an insufferable swine. 'You were married and you didn't tell me!' she said, barely controlling her voice. 'That's why you didn't...didn't want to...' To her horror, tears filled her eyes. 'When I found that picture I thought...I thought you'd *lost* them! I thought that something terrible had happened to them. But that's not the way it was, was it?'

His face turned to stone. 'I fail to see why I should discuss my private life with you, Livia. For God's sake, what does it matter to you now?'

Tears ran down her face. 'It matters because I don't like to be deceived! I don't like being lied to!' She took a deep, steadying breath. 'Right before I came here,' she said, her voice quivering, 'somebody told me your wife had died.' She kept her eyes trained on his face.

Nothing happened. No shock, no guilt, nothing. His expression remained unchanged. 'Yes, she did,' he said calmly.

She stared at him. 'You know?'

He shoved his hands into his shorts pockets. 'Of course I know! Why wouldn't I know my own wife died? It happened almost five years ago.'

She stared at him, uncomprehending. She hadn't heard right. She was going crazy. 'Five years ago?' she whispered.

'Yes.'

His wife had died five years ago. Tammy's mother had died recently. Something was wrong. Something was terribly wrong. She felt suddenly hopelessly lost.

'I don't understand,' she said. 'What about the baby? The baby on the picture?'

His face worked and there was a flash of bitter pain in his eyes. He picked up a stick and threw it viciously into the underbrush. 'The baby wasn't ours,' he said.

CHAPTER EIGHT

LIVIA'S mouth went dry. It was hard to breathe. Cold apprehension slithered through her. Clint turned abruptly and walked back to the fire.

She stared dazedly at his broad back straining under the black T-shirt. If Tammy was not his child, then who was she? Why did she think he was her father? Was all this some awful mistake and had she come all the way over here for nothing?

And why was Clint so obviously distraught answering her questions? She looked at his back as he poked around in the fire. Don't ask any more questions, his back said. Leave me alone.

Two long, tiring hours later they stopped for lunch, which consisted of fresh river fish, rice, and roasted bamboo shoots. Livia wished she could lie down and sleep for the rest of the day, but stoically got to her feet again and put on her backpack. It felt as if it were filled with rocks. She gritted her teeth. She was here voluntarily and she was not going to complain. Not in a hundred years.

After an endless afternoon stumbling and tripping along the damp, leech-ridden trail, they stopped at a spot the two guides considered a good camping site. The sweat-bees had come out in droves, and she kept swatting at her legs to get rid of them. The men built a fire and went in search of material to build a sleeping platform for the night. The air vibrated with the maniacal shrieking of the cicadas and Livia listened numbly as she sat by the fire, too exhausted to move even the smallest muscle.

The *pondok* built, the two men took a gill net and walked a little further along the riverbank to do some fishing for the evening meal. 'We'll have our baths now,' Clint said to Livia. 'Let's go.'

The water was cold and crystal-clear and she ducked under several times to cool off completely. She tried not to look at Clint standing there like Adam in paradise, his strong body silhouetted against the dark forest as he soaped himself. It was all too intimate standing here together, washing off the day's perspiration and dirt. She tried to make quick work of it, cursing at the annoyance of the wet sarong around her.

'Take the thing off,' he said. 'They're out of sight.'

'No.'

His brows arched. 'What do you think I'll do?'

She gritted her teeth. 'I just don't feel like standing naked in front of you. It's as simple as that.'

He shrugged as he shampooed his hair. 'Suit yourself.'

It wouldn't bother him if she had nothing on. He'd seen all there was to see and he was no longer interested in her, so what was the big deal?

With one hand she ripped the wet cloth off and flung it on to the big rock where her clothes and towel lay. It was a relief to have it gone. Waist-deep in water, her back turned to him, she washed, shampooed and then ducked under to rinse. It felt wonderful.

She came up for air and swung her dripping hair back and caught Clint's gaze on her. For a moment they stared at each other and her breath caught in her throat. Then he ducked under and rinsed off.

It had been a moment only, a fraction of time, but the look in his eyes had betrayed him. He might not want her to stay. He might be angry that she was here, but he was still affected by her.

Lust, it was only lust. That was all it had ever been. She gritted her teeth and waded back to the rock, drying herself off with her back turned to him. Wrapping a dry sarong around her, she sat down to towel her hair dry. The river water was cold and the sun felt good on her cool skin.

She leaned her head forward and squeezed the water out of her hair, then tossed it back and rubbed it with a towel.

Clint had climbed out as well and was sitting on a rock near by, a towel wrapped around him. He was looking at her legs, which were scratched and bruised, but it was a purely clinical look. Clint was a master of control. 'I'm a man of great self-restraint,' he had said once.

'You need some ointment on those scratches,' he said with cool detachment.

'I know. I have some.' She had anti-bacterial stuff in her bag. She had no intention of getting tropical ulcers if she could help it.

Clint leaned back on his hands and lifted his face to catch the sun. She watched him, seeing the taut muscles in his arms, the strong column of his neck, feeling again the treacherous sensations creeping through her blood. She turned her head and squeezed her hair hard.

A cloud of brightly coloured butterflies danced above the water near by. Mesmerised, she watched them until they fluttered out of sight. She'd never seen so many together. Everything around her was spectacularly beautiful—the orchids dripping from the huge trees, the bright orange fungus growing on a dead log, the lovely bird song in the air. She glanced back at Clint, who was still leaning back on his hands, his eyes closed.

They were alone. No sign yet of the men. All afternoon the question of who Tammy was had haunted her. It had twisted and swirled around in her mind, making her crazy. She needed to know.

She took a fortifying breath. 'Clint?'

He opened his eyes and looked at her. 'Yes?'

'I know you don't want to discuss your private life with me, but would you please tell me one thing? That baby in the picture...'

He leaned forward, taking his weight off his arms, and gave a sigh of exasperation. 'Livia——'

'If she wasn't your child, who was she?'

He rested his forearms on his drawn-up knees. There was a silence as he stared off into the verdant greenery of the forest. 'She was my wife's niece, her sister's illegitimate baby,' he said tightly. 'My wife and I took care of her for a year. And before you ask me why, it was because the baby's mother had a lot of problems. Alcohol-related.'

Oh, God. Livia's heart contracted. It fit perfectly with the bits and pieces Tammy had told her.

'What happened after that year?'

'Her mother took her back.' His voice was flat, emotionless. He kept staring off into the trees, not looking at her.

'Just like that?'

He looked at her then. 'No, dammit, not just like that!' He raked his fingers angrily through his wet hair. 'Do you think for a moment that I let her go voluntarily? That I loved and nurtured a child for a year and then simply gave her up? What kind of man do you think I am?' His eyes burned into hers. It was as if a sudden spark had ignited a fire inside him. 'Do you think I make my commitments lightly? I went through the courts, the whole damned route, until there was no further to go. The plain and simple facts were that I had no rights. I was not the father. I was no blood relative at all, and my wife had recently died. The mother said she'd sobered up and wanted her back, and they gave her to her.' He glared at her. 'And that, Livia, was the end of my family.' He slipped off the rock and climbed on to the riverbank.

She didn't follow him immediately, but watched as he dragged on a set of clean clothes, noticing the strain in his forceful movements, the rippling of his muscles. Her heart ached and his final words kept echoing in her head. 'And that, Livia, was the end of my family...'

My family... The family she had seen on the picture—a loving wife, a happy baby. Gone. Finished. She swallowed at the constriction in her throat.

Back by the fire he made tea and offered her a mug in a calm, businesslike manner, yet she could sense the tension thick between them. He hadn't wanted to talk about his past, but he had, and now it was all back in his consciousness where very obviously he didn't want it to be. She couldn't help feeling guilty and she didn't dare touch the subject again.

She drank the hot tea, wishing she had a long tall glass of lemonade with ice cubes instead, but that was not within the realm of possibilities.

She took a tube of anti-bacterial cream from her bag and screwed off the cap.

'Let me have a look at this,' Clint said, holding out his hand.

She dropped the tube into his hand, not touching him.

He examined the tube. 'It'll have to do. Let me see your leg. Put your foot on my knee.'

'I can put ointment on my own legs,' she said tightly.

'I know you can, but I want to make sure there's nothing there that needs other treatment.' He shifted position, picked up her foot and settled it unceremoniously on his knee. He examined the scratches and bruises on the ankle and calf of one leg, then the other.

'Not a pretty sight,' he commented. 'Does it hurt?'

'Not too bad,' she lied. She was determined not to complain. The cuts stung and throbbed.

'Nothing serious, though.' He squeezed out some ointment and began to spread it around, his touch surprisingly gentle. He was so close that she could smell the soapy scent of his skin. She felt suddenly terribly fragile as if she could shatter in a thousand pieces with one wrong move or one wrong word. She felt wrung out—physically as well as emotionally. It hurt to be so close to him, yet feeling as if oceans separated them. It hurt to remember the closeness they had once shared. It hurt to feel this aching need to touch him, to feel his heart beating against her. She wanted to tell him she was sorry about all the terrible things she had thought about him.

She loved him. Tears came to her eyes and she bit her lip hard.

He looked up, meeting her gaze. 'Livia?'

His face was a blur and she lowered her gaze to stare blindly at her hands clenched together in her lap.

'I'm sorry I hurt you,' he said softly.

She swallowed with difficulty. For a fleeting moment she wondered if he was talking about her legs, or if he had sensed that her tears had nothing to do with physical pain.

'It's all right,' she said huskily. 'I'll live.'

But she wasn't so sure if that was true.

She couldn't sleep. The *pondok* floor was hard and uneven. She kept seeing Tammy's face, the eagerness in her eyes. She kept hearing her voice. 'Will you help me find my father?'

Would he want her back now? But how could that be? A child would fit his lifestyle even less than a wife would.

What was going to happen to Tammy? What would happen to her when she found out Clint was not her father? Was there any other place for her to go? It hadn't seemed like it.

Clint lay next to her, all but touching, the flimsy netting of the mosquito screen separating them.

Clint, who hadn't deserted a wife and child. Clint, who had selflessly loved someone else's baby, who had done everything in his power to get custody of her after his wife had died.

Her head ached. Her heart ached. She'd jumped to all the wrong conclusions, made premature and un-informed judgements, all the things an intelligent person shouldn't do. Her emotions had taken over and her brain had closed down. She had even mis-trusted her own judgement of him—that he was a good, caring man with strong principles.

She wished more than anything she dared sneak her hand out from under the netting, touch him, tell him she was sorry she'd thought such evil things of him. Only he didn't even know she had. All he knew was that she was here, that he didn't want her here, and that she was prying into his private life.

She turned over and the sapling platform creaked and swayed. There was the scent of the smoky fire the other men kept going to keep the mosquitoes away, and the strange noises from the forest—shrieks and rustlings and cries.

'You're not sleeping,' Clint said in a low voice.

'No.' And neither was he, obviously. By the sound of their breathing it seemed the other two men were fast asleep.

Clint swore softly. 'Livia, please understand. I can't offer you what you're looking for. You can't stay here with me. I can't come back. I can't offer you any kind of commitment. Not you, not any woman.'

'Why not?' she whispered, feeling a desperate ache in the pit of her stomach.

'Because nothing lasts.' The words seemed wrung out of him. 'Because I don't know how to live for the future. Permanency doesn't fit into my lifestyle.'

Not if you don't want it to, she replied silently. He thought she'd come here to be with him. Well, why should he think anything else? She hadn't yet told him of the real reason. It was getting harder and harder to do. She could tell him now, blurt out the truth; I came to tell you that there's a little girl looking for you. A little girl who thinks that you are her father. She wants to live with you in the rainforest. Her tongue wouldn't move, as if some invisible power was holding back her words.

'Go to sleep, Livia.'

As if it were that easy. Go to sleep.

But in the end it was easy. She was physically and emotionally drained and nature had mercy on her and gave her oblivion. She tumbled into an exhausted sleep, deep and dreamless until the ascending whoop-whoop-whoop-whoop cries of gibbon monkeys awakened her.

Clint stirred next to her and she glanced at his body relaxed in sleep, then quickly averted her gaze and stared up at the leafy roof of the *pondok*. The two porters had left the sleeping shelter and she heard their muted voices by the fire. She lay with her eyes open and listened to the sounds of the forest coming to life—the joyful warbling of birds, the cries and shrieks of unseen creatures in the greenery. A thin beam of golden sunlight struggled through the canopy.

Next to her Clint sat up and raked his fingers through his hair.

'Good morning,' he said.

'Good morning.'

'How did you sleep?'

'Fine,' she said. As fine as you could sleep on an uneven sapling floor. Her every muscle ached, but not a complaint would cross her lips.

'How do your legs feel?'

'They're all right. I'll put more stuff on them before we go.'

How polite. How civilised. Her stomach cramped, but it wasn't from hunger. She remembered those other mornings waking up next to him—his hand reaching for her, drawing her close to his warm, aroused body.

He was staring at her, his eyes inscrutable, yet she sensed that behind the composed expression he remembered too. She saw the sudden subtle tensing of his body. She closed her eyes, blocking out his face, trying to banish the memories. A moment later she felt the swaying of the platform as he was climbing down. She heard the soft thump as his feet hit the ground.

They walked all day, along a jungle path that followed the rocky river, which was a narrow stream tortured with rapids. It was so exhausting that she had no strength for talk. She refused to complain. She didn't feel like talking. She'd have to wait till they got to the longhouse village to find a time to tell him.

She felt warm and sticky and she kept smelling the insect repellent she'd rubbed into her skin. The jungle closed in on her, suffocating. The warm, moist air was hard to breathe. She knew the men were keeping their pace down to accommodate her slow and inexperienced pace, and she was annoyed by her own inept movements.

Yet there was so much beauty and at times she would forget her miseries and simply be awed by the huge ferns, the thick, knotted vines crawling up the trees, the myriad mushrooms and other colourful fungi. High, high above stretched the green canopy, blocking out most of the sun. Gibbon monkeys swung from trees. Brightly coloured birds fluttered from branch to branch.

Late in the afternoon they reached the village and were greeted happily by the people just returning from their garden plots. It was a joy to see people, to see their smiling faces, to see the azure sky above the longhouse clearing.

Clint leaned his head towards her as they climbed the pole ladder. 'I'm going to introduce you as my wife,' he said. 'For propriety's sake.'

She thought her heart had stopped. 'For propriety's sake?' she repeated. 'Why?'

'You'll have to stay in my room. There's no room anywhere else unless you want to sleep with half a dozen girls and children crowded in one room. Nobody would mind, but I thought you might.'

She swallowed. 'Thank you.'

Clint introduced her to Pak Lampung, the headman, a dignified old man who gave her a sharp, intelligent look and smiled in welcome. She had the uncanny feeling that he didn't believe for a moment that she was Clint's wife, but was too polite to say anything about it. Children crowded around them. Clint laughed, took out a bag of sweets from his backpack and handed them out, going down on his haunches as he talked to the kids.

They climbed up the pole ladder to the veranda and a tall blond man approached them with a wide grin. With his eyes on Livia he pressed his hand to his heart.

'Ah! A vision!' he said.

More like a nightmare, Livia thought, but laughed at his exaggerated greeting. She'd never felt more like something that had crawled out of a swamp in her life. She was sweaty, messy, scratched and bruised, and smelled of bug repellent.

The man glanced over at Clint. 'And where did you find this lovely creature?' he asked. 'You didn't tell me you'd put her on the supply list.'

Clint's face was impassive. 'It's one of those little surprises in life, my friend,' he said evenly. 'Livia, this is David Holloway, my partner. David, meet Livia Jordan. She's passing through.'

His hand was rough and strong as he grasped hers. His blue eyes smiled into hers. 'It's very nice to meet you, Livia,' he said solemnly. He turned back to Clint and frowned. 'Didn't I hear you mention a Livia? Is she the wonderwoman remodelling your grand-mother's house?'

'Yes.' Clint's voice was terse. 'And the under-standing here is that she's my wife.'

'Lucky you.' Reluctantly, David let go of Livia's hand. 'How long are you staying?'

'Till the next supply plane leaves,' she said, and David arched a surprised brow. She followed Clint and the people carrying their things to a door at the end of the wide veranda.

Clint opened the door which led into a dark room. He went inside and propped open several window shutters hinged at the top to let in the light, and Livia glanced around. Piles of books, papers, a table with a typewriter, hooks from which hung clothes, shelves with boxes, jars and cans and several bottles of Scotch. The floor was bare hardwood. Someone carried in her backpack and put it down on the floor. The porters brought in the boxes with supplies and left.

Clint raked his hands through his hair and glanced around the room. 'We'll move things around to make room for your mat later. We've been invited to have drinks and dinner with the headman tonight. This is the bathroom, if you want to wash. We'll go to the river before dinner.'

He showed her the alcove screened off by rattan matting. Removable slats revealed an opening in the floorboards. A bucket of water with a plastic dipper stood underneath a small stand which held a few toiletries—a razor, toothpaste. A small mirror hung above it.

The evening was a repeat of the one she'd spent in the trading-post longhouse. The wide communal veranda was crowded with people talking and laughing. There was food, plenty of *arak*, story-telling, music and then dancing.

She was numb with fatigue. She escaped to Clint's room, making space by pushing things around and rolled out her mat on the hardwood planks. Having brushed her teeth and tended to her abused legs, she rigged up her mosquito net and went to sleep. It didn't matter that the floor was hard. Nothing mattered but being horizontal.

Again that night, she slept like the dead. She didn't think she'd ever feel rested again.

She awoke the next morning, feeling cold. Clint was up and had made a fire in the indoor fireplace. Steam rose from a water kettle. She had not heard him come in during the night; she hadn't even heard him stirring around making the fire. She sat up on her mat and pushed her hair out of her face.

'Good morning,' he said. 'Coffee'll be ready in one more minute.'

'Thank you.' She pulled the mosquito net aside. 'It's cold. I didn't know it could get so cold here.'

'It's the altitude, and it rained last night. Didn't you hear it?'

She shook her head. 'No. I was tired. I didn't hear anything.' She retied her sarong and moved closer to the fire.

Clint spooned instant coffee into two enamel mugs and poured water. He handed her one of the mugs. 'Here you go. We'll have breakfast with David in a little while.'

It was all so quiet, so polite. Well, she had no energy for anything else. She sipped the hot coffee, listening to the sounds from the awakening forest.

She was relieved when David joined them a few moments later, his easy smile lightening up the atmosphere. Breakfast was served by a neighbour lady, who'd taken on the job of seeing to the men's daily food needs. She was a friendly, talkative grandmother of many, with heavy brass rings weighing her earlobes down to her shoulders.

The food was delicious and, as she ate, Livia imagined herself climbing up and down ladders, painting or hanging wallpaper, with brass earrings hanging from her extended earlobes. It would drive her crazy really fast. Then again, if you grew up with the things you wouldn't know any better. She wondered if the women took them out at night, or just flopped them around in bed with them. It seemed they'd get in the way, or do physical damage to a lover. The thought made her grin.

After breakfast, David went back to his room to work and Clint got ready to take off for the day. He didn't say where.

'I'll be gone all day,' he said. 'Stay at the house. Don't go wandering off on your own, you understand? Ten steps off the path and you may be lost forever.'

She didn't mind resting and she was relieved when he left. Being with him for the past three days had been a severe strain on her nervous system, her heart and her patience.

The longhouse was quiet in the morning with most of the villagers having left to work their *ladang*. She watched an old woman husking rice with a five-foot hardwood pole, and she played with the children, who thought she was the best thing since sliced bread. She realised that it was the first time in days she had laughed. This was not a happy thought. She liked laughing. If you couldn't laugh any more, things were seriously wrong.

Things *were* seriously wrong.

She had lunch with David, cooked by the old woman—rice and fresh river fish, and some stir-fried fern tendrils and wild mushrooms. He was working on traditional medicine, he explained. He had catalogued an enormous number of different plants and trees from the forest whose roots, flowers, leaves and bark were used to make medicine. He was preserving specimens in the plant presses he had in his room and documented their preparation and use.

Soon after lunch several men came out of the forest with a huge boar they had shot. She made herself watch as they butchered the animal, telling herself that this was part of the reality of village life here, and an experience for her to chalk up. However, it was not a pretty sight, and one that might convince her to try vegetarianism. The butchered meat was spread out on a rack built over a big, smoky fire where it would remain overnight. Smoking the meat, she was told, would keep it good for several days.

At the end of the afternoon people came back from their garden plots and everyone went bathing in the river.

By sunset Clint came back and headed straight for the river to bathe. After he returned, the three of them had dinner in David's room and the men talked about their work. David drew her into the conversation several times, but Clint paid her little attention past the normal civilities and she felt a toxic mixture of resentment and despair.

After dinner they socialised on the longhouse veranda, where storytelling was the major form of entertainment. For a while her miseries seemed pushed back by the enjoyment of the moment—the fun-loving people, the laughter, the stories. In spite of everything, she was happy she had come.

When everyone started drifting off to their family quarters, Clint came to his feet and she followed him back to his room.

He lit a candle and a soft light spread around the room. He held the same match to a green mosquito coil which sent off a spiral of incense-scented smoke.

They were alone and she knew she could no longer postpone telling him about Tammy. She sat down on her mat and put her hands in her lap.

'There's something I need to tell you,' she said quietly. 'I've been waiting for the right moment, but I don't think there is one, so I might as well do it now.'

He raised his brows. 'What?'

She looked at him, unwavering. 'I know you think I came here because I wanted to be with you,' she went on. 'It's understandable for you to think that.'

'And you didn't?'

'No, I didn't. I have more pride than that, Clint.'

Hands in his pockets, he observed her silently. 'Then what was the reason?'

She wished he would sit down. He loomed over her, making her feel small and vulnerable. 'There's a probl . . . situation you need to know about and there wasn't time to wait until a telegram would catch up with you two months from now. So I got on a plane. It was the only way I could think of to reach you quickly.'

He grew very still. His face lost all expression. 'Are you telling me you're pregnant?' he asked tonelessly.

Stunned, she stared up at him. It hadn't at all occurred to her that he might think that. She shook her head. 'No, oh, no. We were careful. We never took any risks.'

'There are always risks,' he said tersely. 'There are no guarantees.'

'No.' Not in anything. She stared at him, her mind suddenly wild with questions. What if she had been pregnant? What would he have done?

'If I had been pregnant,' she asked softly, 'what would you have done?'

He raked an impatient hand through his hair. 'I don't know, Livia. It's a hypothetical question at this point, and not one I want to dwell on. Now what's the point of this conversation? What was so important that you needed to come all the way over here?' He sat down on the chair at the table. The candle flickered, throwing wild shadows across the room. A frenzied shrieking came from the forest.

She was not sure how to tell him, so she decided to dive right in. She took a steadying breath.

'Somebody delivered Tammy to the house and said it was time for you as her father to take responsibility for her upbringing. Her mother died recently.'

Under his tan all colour drained from his face.

'*Tammy*?' His voice was rough.

She nodded. 'That's the girl in the picture, isn't it? Only she's not a baby any more. She's six.'

He closed his eyes briefly. 'Oh, my God,' he muttered. He composed himself with an effort. 'Her mother is dead?'

'Yes. A neighbour brought Tammy to me.'

'Where did they come from?'

'Pennsylvania.'

'I couldn't find them,' he said tonelessly. 'Where is she now? What did you do with her?'

'She's at Jack and Sara's. They've got two girls of their own; you met them at my birthday party. She'll love it there. They're going camping and she was so excited about it and——' She bit her lip and stopped the stream of words.

He looked more tired than she had ever seen him. 'That woman who was with her said I was Tammy's father?'

'Yes.'

He gave a bitter laugh. 'God, the irony. I wonder where she got that idea.' His voice held sarcasm.

Tammy's mother must have told her he was the father. She must have told Tammy the same thing. How else could she have known the facts that she had?

'Why would Tammy's mother lie about it?'

'Because she didn't know who had fathered Tammy, and she probably needed a story. I was convenient— far away and out of reach.' He gave her a sharp look. 'And Tammy? What does she think?'

Her heart lurched. 'That you are her father. And she wants to live with you in the jungle. That's what she said.'

He rubbed his face. 'So that's why you were asking me all the questions,' he said tonelessly.

'Yes. And you thought I wanted to dig into your past to find out some deep and hidden psychological reason why you don't want me.'

He winced at her words. 'It's not that I don't want you, Livia,' he said roughly. 'For God's sake, you should know that.'

Her heart lurched. He wanted her, but not the way she wanted to be wanted. She bit her lip and said nothing.

His face was grim. 'And you also thought I was Tammy's father, of course.'

She shrugged lightly. 'I had no reason to think otherwise. I came here ready to tell you what a despicable excuse of a man you were to abandon your own child. I had it all worked out in my head. It was quite a speech.'

A glimmer of a smile curved his mouth. 'Sorry to spoil your fun.' He rose and massaged his neck. 'What does she look like?' he asked.

She hesitated. 'She's thin. Longish blonde hair. Big grey eyes.' Wise eyes. Not the eyes of a child.

He looked at her sharply. He had noticed her hesitation. 'What's wrong with her?'

She sighed. 'She doesn't…she doesn't look like she was well cared-for. I think she's had a hard life for a kid her age.'

She saw anger flare in his eyes. His hands balled into fists. He turned and without another word he walked out of the door, back on to the veranda.

She got ready for bed, lay down on her mat and stared up into the thatched roof, wondering what he was thinking, what he was feeling.

*   *   *

He worked on his typewriter for the next few days, hammering away on the old portable for hours on end, hardly emerging from the room, hardly speaking to her at all. At night he would not come into the room until late, thinking she would be asleep. Sometimes she was, sometimes she wasn't.

'Is there anything I can help you with?' she'd asked, but he had said no. She had more success with David, who was more than pleased to have her proofread some of the material he had written or retype some of the edited copy. Along with his medicinal flora, he had also collected a wealth of legends, superstitions and other interesting tales dealing with illness and disease. She was fascinated reading them and talking to him about them over lunch. Clint would say little, keeping the conversation purely professional, which would mostly exclude her. He'd eat quickly and go back to his room without lingering.

'He's not a happy camper these days,' David commented one afternoon. He observed her intently. 'I thought he'd be delighted to have you here.'

'He isn't,' she said, and glanced down at her plate.

'Most women I know would think I'd be out of my mind if I suggested they come to see me here. You've got guts, Livia.'

'More guts than sense, probably,' she said with a wry smile.

That night after dinner Clint followed her into the room. 'I want to ask you some questions,' he said, putting his hands in his shorts pockets. 'That woman who brought Tammy to the house—what exactly did she say?'

The question took her by surprise. He hadn't mentioned Tammy after she had told him about her—not a single word. It wasn't hard to remember what the woman had said; it hadn't been much, so it didn't take long to tell him. He was watching her as she spoke, his face dark and brooding.

'Did she say why Janine...Tammy's mother died?' he asked.

'No. Tammy mentioned something about helping with the housework because her mother was often sick.'

He cursed under his breath and his hands clenched in anger. 'It's not hard to guess why. I imagine she'd hit the bottle again.' His voice was hard and his eyes looked somewhere in the distance, seeing things, remembering things.

'Tammy has a teddy bear,' Livia said softly. 'She said her daddy gave it to her.'

There was something terrible in his eyes, a mixture of grief and rage that shook her to the core. 'What else does she have?'

'Nothing much. Some clothes, a doll, a snapshot of you and her when she was learning to walk.'

His jaw worked. 'What else has she said about me? What does she know? She was too little to remember anything.'

'I overheard her talking to her bear when she was going to sleep. She said you're a famous scientist doing very important work and that one day you would come back.' She swallowed at the lump in her throat. 'I think she's woven an enormous fantasy around you.'

He slammed his fist against the wall, then leaned his forehead against the wood. 'I'll have to go back to sort things out,' he said tonelessly. 'Are you sure she's all right with your brother and sister-in-law for now?'

'She couldn't be in better hands. They'll keep her as long as necessary and give her lots of TLC.'

He met her eyes. 'Thank you for going through all this trouble, Livia. I appreciate it.'

She saw again Tammy's earnest face, the solemn grey eyes, heard the worried voice: 'Will you help me find my father?'

'I had no choice, Clint.'

'Oh, sure you did. You could have passed her off to the authorities and let them worry about contacting me. And, knowing that I'm not her father, they might not have contacted me at all.' He straightened away from the wall. He looked big and tall in the confines of the room.

She took a deep breath. 'What are you going to do?'

'I'm going home to sort things out. I'll take the next plane out. We can travel back together.'

The next day, David asked her to go with him to collect a rare plant specimen someone had found in the forest canopy. After several days in the longhouse, she was ready for a little side-trip and the two-hour-long trek through the jungle was hardly exercise now, and climbing up in the canopy with a rope-and-pulley contraption was an exhilarating experience, be it a rather dangerous one. It was a different world up there with plants and vines and animals that never touched ground, but survived off the trees. She enjoyed David's company and he seemed happy to answer all her questions.

They arrived back at the longhouse in the middle of the afternoon and she went for a swim with some of the children. Refreshed and cooled off, she went back to the room to put on some clothes. The long-house was quiet and almost deserted. People had not yet returned from the garden plots and the children were still in the river.

She was squeezing her hair dry when Clint walked in. He did not look happy. In fact, he looked furious.

'I told you to stay in the village!' he said tightly. 'I told you specifically not to wander off! And what do you do? You take off into the forest for the whole damned day!'

She could not believe her ears. 'I hardly wandered off. I was with David.'

'You are my responsibility and I don't want you in the forest!' He pulled his shirt off over his head.

She tried not to look at his brown chest, but settled her gaze on his face. 'I am not your responsibility. I came here on my own account. I am responsible for myself and I'm not an idiot.'

He tossed the shirt on the chair. 'You climbed up into the canopy! What do you call that?'

'I call it an adventure,' she said, trying hard to stay calm. 'It was fantastic, actually.'

He glared at her. 'It was irresponsible and dangerous, that's what it was! And while you are here as my guest, you will damned well do as I say!' He placed his hands on his hips. 'And one more thing. I think you've taken up enough of David's time. I would appreciate it if you could leave him alone so he can get on with his work. Read a book, teach somebody English.'

Stunned, she stared at him, anger rushing through her at his implication. 'Are you saying I'm distracting David from his work?' Her voice shook.

His face was hard, his eyes unreadable. 'I think you should leave him alone.'

'I think David can take care of himself. And if I spend time in his room, then that's because he wants me there! Which is more than can be said for you!' She was shaking with anger. She turned abruptly, ready to leave, but he moved swiftly, took her arm and turned her to face him.

They stared at each other for a frozen moment, silent and without moving, the anger pulsing between them. A muscle moved in his neck. His hand relaxed on her arm. The tension changed almost imperceptibly and the anger shifted until it was no longer anger that throbbed between them, but a madness of another kind, more dangerous, more volatile. She began to tremble, feeling powerless to move away, powerless to utter a sound. Under her feet the floorboards creaked. From outside came the high-pitched warble of a bird. And all around was the rich, earthy scent of the jungle, primitive, pulsing with life.

CHAPTER NINE

CLINT'S hand reached out and lightly touched her cheek. Her heart leaped. 'Livia?' His voice was a husky whisper.

Black fire shone in his eyes and she trembled, yearning, aching, afraid of the dark desire he aroused in her. She looked into his eyes, mesmerised.

'Yes,' she whispered.

She felt his hand on the upper swell of her breast, tugging the sarong loose. She shivered as the soft cloth slid sensuously along her skin and fell to the floor. She stood naked before him, trembling, and then he hauled her close to him and kissed her with such fierce intensity that she thought her heart would stop. A smouldering fire inside her exploded into heat and light and she gave herself up to it.

He ripped off his shorts with one hand, his mouth not leaving hers. They lowered themselves on to his sleeping mat and his mouth and hands hungrily explored her body. Her breathing came on shallow puffs as she touched him back, trembling with need.

Her body ached, pulsing with an ancient rhythm as he kissed her breasts, his hands caressing every part of her. His skin was hot and smooth under her hands, his muscles strong and taut. She felt in the grip of a primal force, wild and magnificent and frightening.

There was no going back. There was no thought, no sense of time. Their mutual wildness carried them away into a frenzied release, shattering illusions.

* * *

He rolled over and sat up, resting his back against the wall. She sat up too, hugging her knees to her chest and lowering her head to rest on them. She could not bear to look at him, and a terrible desolation took hold of her.

She loved him. It should have been the most wonderful thing in the world, yet all she felt was a helpless despair and a terrible need to cry her eyes out. He did not love her.

She took in a deep, shuddering breath. She wasn't going to. She damned well wasn't going to cry. With the terrible tension between them it had been inevitable that this would happen. And she had wanted it, needed it.

She felt his hand on her head for an instant, then he came to his feet. The floorboards creaked as he moved across the room to the veranda door. Then he was gone.

'I'll sleep in David's room,' he said later that evening. 'I should have thought of that earlier.'

Her hands clamped by her side. Her heart ached. She looked at him, saying nothing.

'Don't look at me like that, for God's sake.' His face worked. 'We can't afford to let this happen again, Livia. For more than one reason. One being that there is no pharmacy around the corner and I refuse to play risk-games with fate.'

His gaze lowered to her mouth, then abruptly moved up to her eyes. 'We can't take irresponsible risks, no matter how much we want to.'

'I don't want to at all!' she said hotly, feeling tears stinging her eyes. 'I've never in my life slept around just for the hell of it! And I'm not going to start with you!'

'Then I hope you'll forgive me for sleeping somewhere else,' he said calmly. He picked up his mat and bedding and left the room.

She hated him for his calm control and she'd only barely managed not to scream at him. She covered her face with her hands and gave a low moan.

Alone, she felt the room close in on her. The jungle outside was alive with sounds. Two more nights and they would start the trek back to the trading post. Two days of walking along the jungle path, one day in a longboat on the river. Then the tiny supply plane would fly them out of the forest.

She felt as if she was living a nightmare.

The night before they left the village, there was a goodbye party with traditional dancing, music making and lots of rice wine and *arak*, of which she only took a few sips. She'd need all her strength for the trip back to the trading post. Several men had gone hunting and shot a huge deer, which was butchered and then roasted over a fire. Not exactly your suburban backyard barbecue, but the roasted chunks of meat were delicious.

Two men accompanied them as they set off early the next morning, their rattan backpacks full of goods they would trade or sell at the trading post: birds' nests, aromatic woods, medicinal plants. All of these would be flown to the coast and on to various markets in the Orient.

Clint was more distant than ever, saying little, and preoccupied with his own thoughts, which, by the looks of his expression, were not happy ones. Livia had a thousand questions fermenting in her mind, but she knew he would not welcome them. She felt lonely and left out. She was not part of his life despite the passion they'd shared. He allowed her no entrance to the deepest part of himself.

Millions of coloured lights glimmered and flickered below her in the night—the miracle of modern electricity in all its colourful splendour. Hong Kong. Livia gazed out of the jet window, waiting for the plane to make its dramatic descent to Kai Tak Airport. The buildings were eerily close as the plane made its final approach. Lights flickered in windows, faintly illuminating washing strung on balconies. Traffic rushed by just below.

The landing came fast and smooth, the wheels touching the surfaced runway with hardly a bump.

A sleek limousine delivered them to their hotel, where doors were opened and luggage collected and people smiled as if they were arriving royalty.

She did not exactly feel like royalty in her wrinkled cotton trousers and blouse. The hotel lobby was overwhelming with its huge three-storey picture windows overlooking Victoria Harbour. All was light and space and discreet opulence.

She had protested when Clint had made reservations for the Regent from the house of a friend in Balikpapan where they'd stayed for a night.

'There are plenty of cheaper hotels that are perfectly adequate,' she'd stated.

'Don't worry about it,' he'd said. 'My treat.'

'But it's not necessary! It's decadent!'

'And so very enjoyable,' he'd said evenly. 'Where have you been sleeping the last few weeks?'

'On a mat on the floor.'

'Right. And tomorrow night you will have a soft bed in a luxurious room with a marble bathroom with a sunken tub and lots of bubbles and a bottle of champagne.'

Hearing it said so graphically made her cave in, but she had argued about staying two nights. It was time to go home. One was enough.

'You need the rest, Livia,' he said impatiently. 'You're exhausted. For heaven's sake, don't argue.'

So she hadn't, because he probably was right. Slogging through the rainforest for two days wasn't exactly a stroll in the park, and sitting in a longboat for a day was hardly restful.

So here they were in the lap of luxury. It was like a time warp. Like waking up on another planet. They were escorted to their two-bedroom suite, and even that struck her as crazy. An entire bedroom just for her. All this space for one person. They'd slept in the same longhouse room on mats on the floor, they'd slept close together on sleeping platforms in the jungle, and now they had again their own private space with a large bed and a door to lock. It was, in a way, a great relief.

They'd only just arrived when a trolley was brought in with tea, chocolate bonbons, fruits, all presented exquisitely beautifully, like a work of art. She took a chocolate and popped it in her mouth. It was heavenly. She looked longingly at the rest of them.

However, what she wanted more than chocolate was a long, leisurely bath in the big whirlpool bathtub, enjoying the view of the harbour that even the large glass windows of the bathroom offered. Before she'd managed to retreat to her own bedroom, another knock came on the door and Clint went to open it. She saw his face light up as a woman breezed in. She was tall and glamorous, her beautiful face framed by a thick mane of chestnut hair. Wearing a long, elegant evening gown of black and bronze silk, she looked simply stunning. Her wide, smiling mouth revealed perfect teeth, and she threw her arms around Clint, who hugged her back and kissed her cheek.

He grinned. 'Couldn't stay away, could you?'

'Absolutely not! It's wonderful to see you again!' She had a lovely, melodious voice. She turned to Livia and extended a slim hand with long, perfectly polished nails. Her green eyes were openly curious. Clint introduced her to Livia as Aurora Dunbar and Livia smiled politely, feeling grungy and drab next to the fragrant, glimmering woman in silk. Not such a surprise, of course. After two weeks in the jungle, and a day on a plane nobody looked glamorous.

She was on her way to a party, Aurora said, but wanted to stop by to say hello. Tomorrow of course they were coming to her dinner party, no excuses!

Clint inclined his head. 'All right, I won't try.'

'I had your clothes delivered,' Aurora said. 'Did you find them in your closet?'

He said he had. Livia wondered how many supplies of clothes he had hanging in various closets around the world. In Balikpapan at the house of his friend he'd left some clothes for safekeeping as well—a lightweight suit, a pair of trousers and a blazer, a few shirts and a couple of pairs of shoes. Anything that didn't get worn and washed on a regular basis in the damp forest turned green with mildew or was consumed by insects or micro-organisms.

'Well, I'm going to leave you to it,' Aurora said. 'Get some rest, have a massage, and tomorrow you'll be as good as new.' She smiled at Livia. 'I can't wait to hear your stories about Clint's jungle hideout!' With a wave of her hand, she floated out of the door, leaving a faint but luscious fragrance in her wake.

Livia glanced around her luxurious surroundings. Her self-esteem was suffering. She couldn't wait to get out of her clothes and into a tub of scented water. Which was where she found herself a little while later.

The tub was huge. The bathroom was finished in pink Italian marble and one wall was almost entirely glass. She was sitting naked in the tub with bubbles up to her chin enjoying the view of Victoria Harbour and all the glimmering lights of the various crafts and the backdrop of buildings. Definitely not your humdrum bathroom experience.

Forty-five minutes later, wrapped in a soft cotton bathrobe furnished by the hotel, she emerged into the sitting-room. Clint was scribbling on a writing pad, not even looking up as she entered.

She stared at his bent head, wondering what he was doing with so much concentration.

'I'd like to know about this party this woman invited us to,' she said. 'What kind of party is it? What do I wear?'

He looked up now, frowning. 'Something formal, dressy.'

'Great,' she said. 'Just the stuff I packed in my backpack for my trip into the jungles of Borneo.'

'Buy something tomorrow. I'll give you some money.'

She gaped at him. His paternalistic attitude was almost funny. 'This is the nineties. I have my own money, and I'll pay for my own clothes, thank you.'

'I'm the one who got you into this,' he said reasonably.

'I'm getting myself into this. I don't have to go to this party if I don't want to. I don't even know who this woman is and I don't believe I should feel obliged.'

'No,' he said drily. 'You should feel pleased. Not just everybody gets invited to a Dunbar party.' A hint of amusement lingered in his words.

'Now I'm really intrigued.' A drop of water dripped from her hair down her temple. She wiped it off. 'Who is she?'

'An old friend. She's a psychologist and her father is a big-time influential businessman with lavish phil-anthropic urges.' He glanced back down at his notepad.

I'll try not to embarrass you, came the thought, but she swallowed the words. There was no excuse for being childish and immature.

He motioned at the room-service table without looking at her.

'I ordered some more food. Help yourself if you're hungry.' He went back to his writing.

There were fragrant bread rolls, a cheese platter, smoked salmon and French country pâté. She looked at his bent head. He hadn't changed or showered and was still wearing the grey trousers and striped dress shirt he'd worn on the plane. What was he doing?

One thing he was not doing was eating with her. He was too busy, or not interested enough. She stared at the food, her appetite gone.

'I'm not hungry,' she said.

He looked up. 'I'd like to call your brother and sister-in-law,' he said, as if he hadn't even heard what she said. He probably hadn't. 'Would you mind giving me the number?'

He didn't say why he wanted to call, but she assumed it was to tell them when he'd be back in the States.

'I can call, if you prefer.'

'Thank you, but I'll take care of it.'

Because it was his business, he meant. She gave him the number and he reached for the phone on the coffee-table. She moved into the bedroom, but she still heard his voice faintly through the closed door. A few minutes later he called her name and handed her the receiver when she got back into the sitting-room. 'Sara wants to speak to you.'

'Hi,' she said into the phone.

'You've surfaced! Good grief, I was worried about you getting lost in the jungle and devoured by tigers.'

Livia laughed. 'How's Tammy?'

'Just fine, chomping at the bit, though, and can't wait for her daddy to come home. I'm so glad he is. I was worried what to tell her if he didn't come back.'

Livia's heart contracted. So Clint had not said anything to Sara about Tammy not being his child. Well, maybe he didn't think it was anybody's business. After all, he hardly knew Sara.

'We'll be there in a couple of days,' she said.

'How did he take the news?' Sara asked.

'I'm not sure.' She took a deep breath. She could not tell Sara the truth, not with Clint sitting in the next room with the door ajar, not when she knew that if he'd wanted Sara to know he would have told her himself.

'You can't talk,' Sara guessed. 'Is he right there?'

'Yes.'

'Well, let's hope it all works out. Now tell me about Hong Kong. Where are you staying?'

A few minutes later Livia replaced the receiver, her heart heavy. It didn't feel right that Sara didn't know the truth. She worried about Tammy's hopes and dreams, about the shattering disillusionment that might come.

Clint came back into the room, pulling off his tie. He still wore his travel clothes.

'What are you going to do?' she asked.

'About what?'

'About Tammy!'

He frowned impatiently. 'Livia, I can't come up with an answer sitting here on the other side of the world. I don't know anything about the facts, the circumstances and the legalities of the situation. It would be stupid to try and decide what to do without speaking to a lawyer, to start with.'

Well, of course. She gritted her teeth. It sounded all so rational, so logical, as if it were merely a business problem that needed to be dealt with, not the fate of a six-year-old little girl with dreams. She hated him for his cool control.

She turned away. 'I'm going to bed. Goodnight.'

'Goodnight, Livia.'

She awoke in the middle of the night, hearing noises in the sitting-room. A faint sound of voices, then silence. It was almost four, she saw on the bedside clock. Wrapping a robe around her, she opened the bedroom door. Clint was sitting in a chair, a cup of coffee in his hand, his hair dishevelled. He was still dressed. He'd rolled up his shirt sleeves and he looked rumpled and tired, his chin dark and unshaven, his eyes black and weary.

'You haven't been to bed yet?' she asked, stunned at the sight of him still dressed.

'Did I wake you? I'm sorry.' He put his coffee-cup down and rubbed his face wearily. 'I had to make some phone calls.'

Phone calls, in the dead of night? Not local, for sure. He must have been calling the States, where it was still yesterday afternoon. Who had he been calling? Social services? A lawyer? She wanted to ask him, but of course she wouldn't dare pry. It was none of her business. He'd made it perfectly clear he wanted to keep her out of his personal affairs.

'I didn't hear you,' she said inanely, pushing her hair away from her face.

He gestured at his bedroom. 'I was in there. I ordered some coffee and food and it was brought in here.' He came to his feet, moved over to the white-shrouded food cart and poured himself a cup of coffee from the pot. 'Go back to bed, Livia,' he said, his back turned to her.

Go back to bed. Leave me alone. Don't disturb me. I don't want you.

She clenched her teeth to stop herself from saying something terrible, something hurtful and angry. Her throat ached and tears burned behind her eyes. She turned and went back to bed, and mercifully sleep claimed her once more and she didn't wake again until it was well past eight in the morning.

She was supposed to rest from her trip through the rainforest and to gather strength for the long haul back to Washington, but of course she could not stay in the room and lounge around all day. Not in Hong Kong!

She stretched luxuriously in the comfortable bed and contemplated the possibilities for the day. Tonight was the dinner party with the luscious Aurora. First thing she needed was a drop-dead stunning dress. Something supremely sexy and alluring, but with a touch of class. She smiled at the ceiling. It so happened that she found herself in Hong Kong, a shoppers' nirvana. The hotel had its very own luxurious shopping emporium, right there for the convenience of its many illustrious guests. Also attached to it was the World Trading Centre with its hundreds of shops. To make things utterly convenient, she had with her a magic piece of plastic that could make all her dreams come true—at least that was what the commercials on TV insinuated. They never mentioned the nightmares that might follow when the dreams eventually needed to be paid for. However, apart from being a romantic fool, she was also a businesswoman with a good grasp on financial reality.

The reality was that she could afford to buy herself some gorgeous clothes.

She jumped out of bed. 'Hong Kong, here I come!' she said out loud.

She slipped into thin cotton trousers and a sleeveless shirt. Not glamorous, but it would do. At least the trousers covered up her legs which were a mess with their scratches and cuts.

Remembering Aurora's suggestion, she called and made an appointment for a massage later that afternoon, and another one at the beauty salon for a shampoo, a facial and a manicure. This hotel was

having a terrible effect on her. It made her feel like a
hedonist. She grinned at herself as she replaced the
receiver.

Clint was not in the sitting-room. His bedroom door
stood half open and she peeped in quickly, seeing him
sprawled across the big bed, the sheet up to his waist.

Her heart made a painful little leap. She suppressed
the urge to go in and sit on the side of his bed and
run her fingers across his chest and watch him wake
up. It was insanity. Despair churned inside her.
Abruptly she swung out of the door, closing it softly
behind her.

She found the dress before noon.

She looked at herself draped in gorgeous silk and
smiled. Victory! It was long, slinky and knock-em-
dead gorgeous, the jewel colours shimmering
lusciously—amethyst, sapphire-blue, aquamarine,
turquoise and emerald-green mingling in a rich
oriental tapestry design. It left her shoulders bare, and
she contemplated the need for a necklace and earrings
which she didn't have, and the cost of some decent
jewellery.

'You need nothing,' asserted the sales lady. 'You
have an elegant throat; leave it bare. And your hair
is lovely. The dress is decoration enough.'

Livia grinned at the woman, who was a picture of
oriental elegance and beauty, and decided that taking
her advice would save tons of money and rescue her
from financial nightmares.

Livia laughed softly to herself as she changed back
into her street clothes. So she had an elegant throat.
Nobody had ever told her that. Here she was, twenty-
nine, and she hadn't been aware of such a
precious asset!

She bought strappy high-heeled shoes to go with the dress, and some silky, lacy underwear that was too frivolous for words, and a small bottle of sinfully sensuous perfume. Signing charge slip after charge slip, she was feeling wonderfully extravagant. It wasn't in her nature to be this way on a regular basis, but why not enjoy it now that she had a perfect excuse?

A perfect excuse.

Why was she doing this? For her own fun? To compete with the gorgeous Aurora? To impress Clint?

She'd spent the last few weeks in an isolated rain-forest village, sleeping on a hardwood floor, wearing sarongs and eating simple food. She was doing this for herself.

Of course she was.

Her purchases would be delivered to her room and, with several hours to spare before her appointments at the hotel, she decided to take to the streets. She should take a nap, but how could she possibly? She'd sleep on the plane tomorrow.

She took the Star Ferry across to Hong Kong Island and got on a double-decker streetcar. Ah, the streets of Hong Kong! The people, the sounds, the smells, the food! It was all a feast for the senses. Potted plants spilled over from apartment balconies in a riot of colour; washing flapped in the breeze and birds twittered from bamboo cages. Garishly coloured signs advertised goods and services in Cantonese and English. People everywhere, talking and laughing, buying and selling, eating, drinking tea, playing mah-jong or telling fortunes.

It had been five years since she'd been to Hong Kong, and she'd been with Lars, a blond giant of a Norwegian she'd met at her parents' house in Kuala

Lumpur where she'd spent her holidays during her university years.

Ah, Lars! She smiled thinking of him now. She'd been so in love, and being with him here in Hong Kong, on her way back to college in the States, had been the epitome of romance. They'd done all the tourist things—gone to the Peak, taken the sunset cruise in the harbour, visited the temples and the jade market, eaten exotic food at roadside stalls and, of course, had their fortunes told.

They were going to be married, have four children, become very rich and live happily ever after.

Sometimes, even the Chinese were wrong. She smiled as she watched the busy streets outside. Their relationship had been a bit wild and tempestuous. It had been fun and sweet and exciting, but it had not run deep, which had become evident once they'd had to go their separate ways to attend to their separate commitments. Time and distance had quickly evaporated their feelings and they'd never met again, despite all their honest and sincere intentions.

Sometimes that was the way it was.

And other times it was different.

She bit her lip and closed her eyes, leaving the colourful street scenes behind, seeing instead Clint's face. After he'd left Virginia to go back to Kalimantan, not a day had passed without her thinking of him, aching for him. Not a day had passed without her hoping he'd change his mind and tell her he loved her and couldn't live without her. No length of time and distance could ever make her love for him go away.

And who was this Aurora? This woman who had his clothes hanging in her cupboard? A friend, he'd said. A friend who'd invited them to a party.

A woman did not fit into his lifestyle, Clint had said. Certainly a glamorous creature like Aurora didn't fit in. So why were all her instincts set on alert?

Maybe she was his Hong Kong mistress. Maybe Aurora did not demand permanency. Maybe they had an arrangement that suited them both.

Like the relationship he'd had with her at home— no ties, no commitments.

She took a deep breath and opened her eyes again, pushing the disturbing thoughts away—or at least into the depths of her mind from where undoubtedly they'd pop out to disturb her some other time. But not now, not here.

She got out of the streetcar at Bonham Strand, feeling her excitement return as she strolled through the crowded streets, past snake dealers and fruit vendors, rattan shops and street barbers. Herbalist shops sported barrels and baskets full of dried herbs, roots and twigs, wild ginseng and dried seahorses. Rows of mysterious bottled potions lined the shelves— medicines, cosmetics, aphrodisiacs. Butcher shop windows displayed rows of Chinese sausages and pressed duck. There was noise and laughter and colour and she loved it.

After an hour of this she could feel herself begin to wilt. She bought some food from a stall and some three-flower tea and started back to the hotel.

Voices came through the door as she opened it. '... And I'll be more than happy to do it,' said a woman's voice. Livia stepped inside. Clint was sitting on the sofa, and next to him was the gorgeous Aurora. She wore a short white skirt and a kingfisher-blue silk shirt, her chestnut curls tumbling down around her head and shoulders in stylish casualness. She looked cool, chic and lovely. Livia felt hot, sweaty and crumpled. Oh, damn, what was that woman doing here?

She felt her heart twist and turn in her chest. The remnants of a lavish lunch languished on the room-service table, including a half-empty bottle of wine. Unless there were other bottles, she couldn't accuse them of copious drinking.

'Hi,' said Aurora, and smiled.

Livia offered a breezy greeting and an equally breezy smile in return. Clint gave a calm hello, saying he gathered she'd been shopping and that an army of people had been bringing things up. He waved at her bedroom door. 'It's in there.'

'Thanks.' She moved to the door, went in and closed it. She dropped on the bed and stretched out, feeling exhaustion take over. And anger. Impotent, helpless anger. What was that woman doing here?

She was jealous. Of course she was. She loved this man and another woman was spending time with him, having lunch with him, smiling at him with her gorgeous green eyes and sexy mouth. A woman who seemed perfectly nice and perfectly friendly, which made it worse. It didn't even give her the satisfaction of hating her.

It made her hurt and ache. She loved him and he didn't want her. She wanted to scream.

Instead she took a shower and cried.

Then she put on the only summer dress she'd brought, and got ready for her massage and beauty salon appointments. Tonight she was going to look ravishing.

And so she did. She studied herself in the mirror one last time before going into the sitting-room where Clint would be waiting for her.

The massage had done wonders for her body as well as her mind. Her face looked refreshed, her skin soft. Her hair gleamed like rich silk. Her hands with their newly polished nails looked lovely.

And the dress. Ah, the dress was exquisite! It draped her body curves just right, all the way to her ankles. She had never looked more elegantly sexy. She dabbed some of the perfume in various strategic places and drew in a deep breath to steady her quivering nerves.

She opened the door and went into the sitting-room. Clint was standing by the large picture window, taking in the view of the harbour. He was wearing black trousers and a white dinner-jacket that fitted across his wide shoulders perfectly.

He turned when he heard her enter. He'd had a haircut and he looked devastatingly handsome in his formal clothes.

Her heart beat loudly in the silence and for a moment she forgot to breathe. He watched her silently, his dark eyes narrowing slightly. She saw the tension sharpen his features.

'My God, Livia,' he said huskily. 'You look...beautiful.' For a moment she saw the familiar black fire in his eyes. Then it was gone.

'Thank you.' Her voice sounded strange.

'A woman of many faces, appearances,' he said. 'Jeans and sarongs, and now this very glamorous affair.' He smiled faintly. 'The first time I saw you,

you were barefoot in a white nightgown and you looked like an angel.'

'And you looked like the devil.'

'Maybe that's who I am,' he said, his mouth curving faintly.

He didn't look like the devil now. He looked stunningly handsome in his immaculate evening clothes, his hair trimmed, his chin cleanly shaven, the dark glint of desire in his eyes.

His hand reached out to touch her, then dropped back by his side.

'Are you ready?'

He was back in control, businesslike, cool.

She swallowed. 'Yes.'

The affair was held in a hotel on Hong Kong Island and it was glamorous indeed.

'I didn't think of you as the type interested in this type of glitzy affair,' she said to Clint. 'I thought you were a jungle man at heart.'

'Ah, so I am.' Humour glinted in his eyes. 'But Aurora begged me, so what could I do?'

'She doesn't strike me as the begging type. Why are you here?'

'Aurora has friends here who are very interested in meeting a jungle man. They're interested in doing a series of TV documentaries showing the lifestyles of indigenous people living in harmony with their environment.'

'And you, of course, will be happy to talk to them,' she concluded.

His mouth twitched. 'Of course.'

The party, as it turned out, was not merely a lavish congregation of Hong Kong's rich and famous for the purpose of eating, drinking and talking business. It was a fundraiser for one of Aurora's father's civil-minded projects—the gutting and remodelling of an entire city block in a squalid neighbourhood on the island. Since Livia also was in the remodelling business, be it on a more modest scale, she had no trouble making conversation. She could talk demolition, plumbing and roofing like a pro.

Aurora, resplendent in white silk, was the perfect hostess. She introduced the two of them around. She also smiled and talked a lot to Clint. Obviously, she very much enjoyed his company. Obviously, Clint very much enjoyed her company. They made each other laugh.

They made her want to cry. Livia's throat ached with the effort not to.

She should not have come to the party. She was not up to this. Once she and Clint had made each other laugh. They'd talked. They'd enjoyed each other's company. Nothing seemed left of that happy, loving time. He did not want her in his life. Somehow she had to come to terms with that.

She slipped away from Clint's side and mingled on her own. She smiled and talked and laughed and drank champagne. There were plenty of other men in the world.

It was still early when Clint came to find her. 'We'd better go back. We have a flight to catch tomorrow,' he said.

She was happy enough to leave. Aurora touched her cheek with her own as they said goodnight. Livia watched as Aurora hugged Clint. 'See you soon,' she said.

CHAPTER TEN

IT WAS almost twelve midnight the following Sunday when they drove up the driveway in the car Clint had rented at Washington Dulles airport. Livia was tired and numb and felt dead inside. All the long, miserable haul home she'd worked at feeling nothing, trying not to hear Aurora's parting words echoing in her head, trying not to be hurt by Clint's reserved manner. He'd been polite and courteous and that was it. A stranger. When they'd talked it had been about impersonal matters. He hadn't mentioned Tammy once.

Whenever she thought of Tammy, her own feelings were pushed instantly to the background. The plight of the little girl overshadowed everything. Being six years old and alone in the world was a cruel fate. If only she could do something, help in some way. But Clint had not told her what he was planning to do and he had not asked for her involvement.

They'd had a wait of several hours in San Francisco and Clint had taken her to the VIP lounge where he'd spent the entire time on the phone while she skimmed through newspapers and drank coffee and watched CNN on the TV set.

Now, finally they were home. The porch light was on, as was a small lamp in the front hall, activated each night by a timer she'd installed before she'd left. It was not a good idea to make a house look deserted, and even here in the countryside she'd not wanted to take any chances.

The house had the impersonal smell of paint and new building materials and stale air. Clint switched on several more lights and glanced around.

'You made a lot of progress. Looks good.'

'Thank you.' She made for the stairs with her backpack. 'I'm going to bed. Goodnight.'

'Goodnight, Livia.'

He was gone in the morning. A note on the kitchen table said he did not know when he would be back, but not to count on dinner.

She heated a frozen breakfast burrito and spent a couple of hours doing paperwork and making phone calls to suppliers and inspectors, then called Sara.

'I'm back,' she said. 'Everything all right?'

'Everything is fine,' said Sara, but there was an odd note in her voice.

'What's wrong?'

'Clint just called a few minutes ago. I told him I'd be happy to drive Tammy over to the house this afternoon, but he asked if we could postpone it for a couple of days and he'd let me know. He was very polite and thanked me for having her and all that.' She paused. 'He didn't exactly sound like a father excited to see his long-lost daughter, Liv.'

Well, he isn't, Livia said silently, but something made her not voice the thought. If Clint hadn't told Sara the truth, it was no business of hers to do so.

'It's a complicated situation,' she said evasively. 'And he's tired. We flew back from Hong Kong without a stopover.'

'You must be exhausted yourself.'

'I'm OK. Ready to start painting again.' There was nothing to do but go on. Finish the house. Buy another one and do it again and plan for another adventurous trip. Somewhere cold. Somewhere without tropical jungles. Alaska. Antarctica.

Sara laughed. 'Why don't you take it easy today?'

She didn't want to take it easy. She wanted to get the house finished as soon as possible. She wanted to keep herself occupied. She wanted to forget everything as quickly as possible.

Only she wouldn't, and the knowledge terrified her.

After she'd replaced the receiver, she went to one of the bedrooms upstairs and started painting where she had left off three weeks earlier.

But painting wasn't very cerebral work and her mind was full of miserable thoughts that refused to be banished.

She'd already gone to bed when she finally heard Clint's car come up the driveway. His steps moved heavily up the stairs, past her door and into his own bedroom. She wondered for the umpteenth time what he had done all day. She pictured him lying in his bed, awake.

She thought of going to him, getting into bed with him, holding him and asking him not to shut her out of his life. Would he refuse her? Would he tell her to leave?

It would be a desperate, foolish act; she knew it well enough. So she stayed in bed, curled up, her heart aching. It took a long time to fall asleep.

'Listen,' said Sara over the phone, 'the suspense is killing us all, so if you don't mind we'll be on our way now.'

Three days had gone by since they'd arrived home. Livia had seen little of Clint, but he'd called her from someone's office the day before and told her that Sara would bring Tammy to the house the next day. Office noises of phones and keyboards were audible in the background as he spoke. A hundred questions had flitted through her mind, but he gave her no opportunity. He said he'd be back late that night and cut the conversation short in clipped, polite tones.

Livia glanced at the clock. 'Clint went into town but he'll be back by the time you get here,' she said to Sara.

But he was not. Sara's van drove up just before eleven and the kids came tumbling out almost before the car came to a full stop. Sara had brought the gang.

Livia was hugged by her nieces and kissed by Sara while Tammy watched. She wore cheerfully flowered shorts and a sky-blue T-shirt. Her grey eyes looked bright and warm colour bloomed in her cheeks. Her hair had been trimmed in a flattering short cut and, although she was still thin, she looked a hundred per cent better than three weeks ago. Livia felt a lump in her throat. 'How about a hug?' she asked and Tammy's face lit up as she threw her arms around Livia's neck.

'Aunt Sara said you found my dad,' she said, her voice trembling with nervous excitement.

Livia released the small figure and smiled at her. 'I did. He should be here any moment. Did you have a good camping trip?'

Tammy's eyes gleamed. 'It was awesome!' she said. 'We slept in tents and we built campfires and cooked hot dogs on sticks. And we went rafting on the river and Uncle Jack taught me how to fish and I caught a huge one! We even ate it for dinner!'

'That's great.' Livia could barely believe the change in her—the childlike enthusiasm, the bright eyes. She smiled at Sara.

'And I can call them Aunt Sara and Uncle Jack,' Tammy said importantly. 'I've never had an aunt and uncle.' She frowned. 'When do you think my dad will be here?'

'I think I hear his car.' Livia glanced out of the window. 'Yep, there he is.'

Moments later Clint strode through the door.

Sara took her two children and disappeared into the kitchen. Livia, transfixed, watched Tammy, who stood very still, staring at Clint with wide grey eyes.

'Hello, Tammy,' he said quietly, his dark gaze intent on her small face.

Tammy's eyes filled with tears. 'Oh, Daddy,' she whispered, 'I knew all the time you'd come back for me.'

And then she rushed forward and Clint went down on his haunches and stretched out his arms to catch her.

CHAPTER ELEVEN

LIVIA'S eyes filled with tears. She turned and fled into the kitchen.

'What's wrong?' asked Sara, her brown eyes looking worried. 'Why are you crying?' She was pouring lemonade. Her girls were playing outside, oblivious of the little drama inside.

Livia slumped down on a chair and swallowed at the constriction in her throat. 'Tammy thinks Clint's her father,' she said thickly.

Sara put the pitcher on the counter and frowned. 'Yes, of course she does. What do you mean?'

Livia wiped her eyes with a tissue and blew her nose. 'He isn't.'

Sara looked at her wide-eyed. 'Clint isn't Tammy's father?'

Livia shook her head. 'No.' She told Sara what Clint had told her, which was not much more than some bare facts. 'He's her uncle by marriage, I guess. But not a blood relative.'

'Oh, my God,' Sara whispered, lowering herself into a chair as if she wasn't sure her legs would hold her up any more. 'What's he going to do?'

Livia rubbed her face, feeling helpless and angry. 'I don't know. He hasn't told me anything, but I think he's been making arrangements the last few days and that's why he couldn't see her until now.'

'If she finds out he's not her father it will break her heart,' said Sara. 'She's hardly stopped talking about him for three weeks. The kid went through hell with her mother. Not that she said so, but it wasn't hard to guess.'

'Her mother had a drinking problem.'

Sara nodded. 'That's what it sounded like from the things she told us.' She frowned. 'You know, Liv, I did think it was strange the way Tammy talked about Clint, as if he were some sort of god. Her mother had been telling her all this larger-than-life stuff. That's not usually the way it is with divorced mothers living in poverty while their ex-husbands have plenty.'

'Her mother didn't even know who Tammy's biological father was.' Livia stared into her glass. 'I've been thinking about it too. Maybe she felt guilty. Maybe in some odd, convoluted way she was giving Tammy in her fantasies what she couldn't give her in real life. A real hero for a father.'

'And Clint was handy to serve as a model.'

'Yes.' Livia fought back tears. 'You know what Tammy said to him? She said, "Oh, Daddy, I knew all the time you'd come back for me." '

'Oh, God,' Sara whispered. 'I hope he doesn't break her heart.'

From the other room came the sound of Tammy's high, excited voice, and Clint's deeper, calmer one. It was impossible to hear the words, or even guess what they were talking about. Livia hugged herself, her arms tight against her ribs as she listened to the muffled sounds. An odd mixture of emotions gripped her—fear, helplessness, loneliness.

Then only Clint's voice was faintly audible, and Tammy was quiet. Was he telling her the truth? Was he telling her he was not her father and that he could not take care of her because he lived in an isolated rainforest village? Was he telling her he would find another place for her to live?

'I don't know what he intends to do with her,' she said tonelessly. 'He's got almost two years left on his contract, and besides, who says the courts will grant him custody when he's not a blood relative?'

'Didn't he say anything at all about what he wanted to do?'

'He said he needed to know the facts and legalities before making a decision. That's all he said. He hasn't talked to me about it.' She bit her lip. 'It's as if he purposely kept me out of it, Sara.' She closed her eyes briefly. 'No, he *did* purposely keep me out of it. He's been perfectly courteous and perfectly distant.' Making her perfectly miserable.

Sara tucked a red curl behind her ear. 'He didn't even say he wanted to take her if the courts would allow it?'

'No.' Livia shrugged. 'But why would he? He doesn't even want a wife. What's he going to do with a child?'

Sara's hands clenched around her glass. 'We'll keep her as long as necessary,' she said with quiet determination. 'We'll try and do whatever we can, Liv. I don't want her to end up a casualty in the system. She needs a real family more than any kid I know.' She picked up the pitcher and poured more lemonade. 'So I gather things between you and Clint are not ecstatic,' she said, changing the subject.

Livia grimaced. 'He was furious when I showed up. He thought I'd come after him. He doesn't want permanency, he says.' She swallowed. 'He said he can't offer me anything.'

'Well, at least he's honest about it.'

Livia bit her lip and stared numbly at her glass of lemonade. It was true. He had never made a secret of his intentions, or lack thereof. It didn't make it easy. It didn't make it stop hurting.

'But you're still in love with him,' Sara commented.

Livia buried her face in her hands and moaned. 'I should have known better than to fall for him, Sara. I knew he was trouble the moment I set eyes on him.'

'I don't think logical thought processes have much to do with falling in love, Liv. What a rotten situation. And all that because of a house.'

'I wish I'd never bought the stupid house.'

Sara gave a half-smile. 'When you sell it back to him, you should top up the price with an extra charge for emotional distress incurred.'

In spite of herself, Livia smiled. 'I'd planned to paint the walls purple and plant poison ivy in the garden.'

'Now that is truly nasty.' Sara laughed. 'Very good, Liv.'

The children came running in, asking for a drink, and then Clint and Tammy appeared as well and little Tammy was glowing.

'Guess what!' she said, her voice jubilant. 'We're going to the airport tonight! We're going to watch the planes land! I've never been to an airport!'

Sara handed her a glass of lemonade and smiled at her. 'How exciting! You'll get to see how big the planes really are close up. You'll love it. Sit down, sweetheart, before you spill it.'

Obediently, Tammy slipped on to a chair. 'We're going to pick up a friend of Daddy's.' She took a gulp of lemonade. 'She's coming to help us. We have to find a house and everything.' She glanced over at

Livia, her eyes shining. 'Until this one is finished. Daddy says we'll live here after you've finished fixing it all up.'

Livia felt as if someone had knocked the wind out of her. There seemed to be no air to breathe.

Tammy looked adoringly at Clint, then back around the table. 'I said I wanted to live in the rainforest with him, but there are no schools and no TV, but we'll go some time during the summer vacation, maybe next year. I know a lot about rainforests, don't I, Aunt Sara? We went to the liberry... library and we found all kinds of books and...'

Livia stared blindly at her hands holding the glass, willing herself to breathe normally. She glanced up at Clint. He stood, hands in his pockets, a vague smile curving his mouth as he watched Tammy, who kept on talking as if she couldn't stop.

Finally, Tammy took another swallow of her drink, then put the glass down and let out a deep sigh as if she felt relieved to have managed to get all this exciting news off her chest. 'Can I go outside and play?'

'*May I*,' corrected Clint. 'Yes, you may.'

She beamed a smile at him, then rushed back over and threw her arms around his waist and pressed her cheek against his stomach. 'Oh, Daddy, I feel so happy!' Then she turned and ran out of the door, followed by the other two girls.

The children's departure left an awkward silence in the kitchen.

'Have some lemonade, Clint,' said Sara, and handed him a glass, looking straight at him. 'It sounds as if you've decided to take care of Tammy,' she said brightly. 'I'd wanted to tell you that Jack and I would be happy to keep her for a while if that would help you get organised.'

'Thank you,' he said and smiled warmly at her. 'But you've done enough. I'm very grateful for what you've done, and now it's my turn.'

Livia felt her heart ache at the sight of his smile. When was the last time he'd smiled at her with warmth? She couldn't even remember.

'So you're not going back to Kalimantan?' asked Sara.

'No. I was offered a full professorship starting in September and yesterday I was told that I have temporary custody until the legalities can be straightened out for permanent custody. It doesn't look as if there'll be a problem.' He took a swallow of his drink. 'After that, we'll start working on adoption.'

Permanent custody. Adoption. Livia's heart turned over and relief flooded her—a wave of joy that washed away her dark apprehensions. Tammy would be all right.

And suddenly she knew why Clint had waited to see Tammy. He had wanted to have certainty about what to tell her. He had done it to protect her, to not raise false hopes and cause more distress. He had made arrangements to keep her—permanently—not even having seen her since she was a baby.

'Oh, Clint,' she heard herself say, 'I was so afraid you didn't want her.'

It was the first time he looked at her directly with more than a fleeting glance and her heart lurched painfully. For a moment he held her gaze in silence. 'It never was a matter of not wanting her, Livia,' he said then. 'It was a matter of what was possible.'

Why didn't you tell me? she asked silently, still looking into his eyes. Why didn't you let me know how you felt? But the words did not come out. A shuttered look came into his eyes, as if he had heard her silent words. He looked down at the glass in his hands, lifted it to his mouth and finished his drink.

Sara looked at him with admiration. 'I can't believe how fast you got all that organised,' she said.

Clint put his empty glass down on the counter. 'Fortunately I know some good people in strategic places.' He did not sit down, but leaned against the counter, legs crossed at the ankles, hands in his pockets.

He certainly had wasted no time getting his affairs in order. Livia remembered the night in Hong Kong when he'd sat up all night making phone calls, and the hours he'd spent on the phone in the airport VIP lounge in San Francisco.

'What about your project in Kalimantan?' she asked, her voice sounding odd in her own ears. She was afraid to acknowledge the implications of what he had been saying, afraid of the tiny spark of hope that suddenly flickered in the depths of her consciousness.

He shrugged. 'David can handle it by himself until they send someone else. They've got two eager candidates already. So much for being indispensable.' Self-derision coloured his voice.

Livia watched his face, seeing no regret, no resentment in his dark features. It was that simple, was it? He gave up the work he loved, moved back to the States and took on a new job. All that to take care of someone else's child, a child he hadn't seen in years.

She wanted to cry. She wanted to throw her arms around him and tell him she loved him, that she would always love him. She wanted to tell him he was the most wonderful, loving man she had ever met.

Instead she sat motionless on her chair, knowing he would not welcome this. Knowing that even now, he was keeping her at a distance.

We're going to pick up a friend of Daddy's, came Tammy's voice in her mind. She's coming to help us.

Aurora. It had to be Aurora. She clenched her hands around her glass. See you soon, Aurora had said as they'd said goodbye.

What would have been more logical than to ask her, Livia, to help? He and Tammy could have easily stayed here at the house until she'd finished with it. The big work was done. She could have watched Tammy when Clint had to give lectures or presentations. She could have taken Tammy shopping for clothes and school supplies. She could have helped her pick out furniture for her room.

Instead, Aurora was coming.

She'd never felt more rejected in her life. Her heart seemed shattered in a thousand jagged shards and everything inside her hurt.

August was hot and humid and it had not rained for weeks on end. A dull haze faded out the view of the Blue Ridge Mountains. Every day Livia ran the sprinkler system to keep the lawn from drying out and the flowers and plants from perishing altogether. She'd hired a gardener in the spring to do battle with weeds, moles and insects, and to keep the place in tip-top shape. It was.

The house was finished. The sun-room was
beautiful with its Mexican tile floor which she'd laid
herself. The wooden floors gleamed, the paintwork
was immaculate, the windows sparkled. The kitchen
had every modern appliance imaginable, yet was warm
and inviting in an old-world way to match the
character of the rest of the house. The kitchen things
she had saved had been washed and replaced in the
cabinets, and as she had emptied the boxes, she'd
found a plastic baby plate that must have escaped her
notice before.

Standing with the dish in her hands, an image of
Clint swam before her eyes—Clint staring at the
jumble of plates and cups and dishes on the counter,
his face unreadable.

He'd seen this dish and he'd thought of Tammy.

She'd washed the plate and put it in one of the
cabinets where one day he would find it. He could
give it to Tammy to keep.

The pieces of furniture stored in the basement had
been brought up and placed in appropriate locations
around the house. They belonged here, and she could
not take them now. Once she was gone, she wanted
nothing to remind her of this house and the man who
owned it.

She loved this house and all her talents and
creativity had been put to work to make it what it was
now, and it was better than she'd imagined.

She stood in the doorway of one of the bedrooms—the bedroom she'd thought would be perfect
for Tammy—and felt a thrill of pride.

She should not have done what she did—it was not
part of the deal, nor part of the job as a whole.

She'd furnished and decorated it.

She glanced around the room, taking in the romantic canopy bed, the old-fashioned rocking chair, the soft white rug on the oak floor, the white wicker dresser and toy chest. It was a lovely room, a happy bright room in glowing white and sunny yellow. Daisies bloomed on the curtains and bedspread. A poster of an old-fashioned picture with small girls in long white dresses running through a field of daisies decorated a wall. A big, life-size baby doll wearing the little dress she'd found in the drawer in the sewing room lay nestled on the bed amid fluffy ruffled pillows. The daisies embroidered on the bodice of the little dress had inspired her in decorating the room.

She left the door ajar and went back down the stairs, walking through the house as she had done so many times, looking for imperfections, for things forgotten or overlooked.

There was nothing.

The house was ready to be sold. Ready to be furnished and lived in. In her mind she had done that, too—found the right tables and chairs, the right curtains and rugs. Beautiful oriental rugs in jewel colours. Huge comfortable sofas. Large potted plants. Paintings and wall hangings from various places around the world. An entire wall lined with bookshelves.

And in her fantasy she'd live in the house. Not alone, of course, but with Clint and Tammy.

And then she'd get furious with herself for making up this fantasy, for not accepting reality, for hoping like a fool. To make herself feel better, she'd add another thousand dollars to the price of the house. Compensation for emotional distress. It didn't make her feel better.

Three estimates had been made and she'd set her price. A price that was fair for the beautiful piece of property, but that would never cover her emotional investments. No monetary price could ever cover those.

Her hand trembled as she reached for the phone. She knew Clint's number by heart, although she had never dialled it. She had not heard from him since he had left the house with Tammy three weeks ago. It had been sent to her in the post, along with their address, an apartment in Charlottesville, not far from the university.

She punched in the numbers and leaned against the wall, bracing herself, her heart hammering loudly as the phone began to ring at the other end.

'Bracamonte,' came the deep voice, and her heart lurched wildly at the familiar sound of it.

'Clint? This is Livia.' Her body was pressed rigidly against the wall. 'I wanted to let you know the house is finished.' She'd practised the words and they came out automatically, as if someone else spoke them for her, a calm, detached business person imparting some information in a calm detached manner.

An almost imperceptible pause followed her words.

'Livia,' he said then. It sounded like a statement, or the answer to a question. 'I'm glad to hear the house is finished. When is a good time to come and see it?'

'Any time. Just let me know. The paperwork is ready.'

'Excellent. How about tomorrow morning, say ten o'clock?'

'That's fine.' Her knuckles were white from clenching the phone. 'How is Tammy?'

'Doing well,' he said. There was a slight pause. 'And you?'

'I'm fine,' she said, and her voice this time had lost its businesslike tone. She pressed her eyes shut.

I'm not fine, she wanted to say. I miss you. I love you. But of course she could not say these things.

'I'll see you tomorrow, then,' he said. 'I'll bring Tammy.'

'Yes, yes. Of course. Goodbye, Clint.'

She hung up and her legs trembled so badly, she had to sit down and wait until the shaking stopped.

At ten o'clock sharp, a car drove up to the house. It was a new, rugged Jeep Cherokee and it was painted a bright, shiny red. Clint in a *red* car? She couldn't believe her eyes.

Tammy must have chosen the colour, she realised then, and couldn't help a grin even though her heart was in her throat as she watched Clint get out of the vehicle.

He looked so good. So tall and in command, so familiar. It hurt just to look at him. Tammy had emerged from the passenger side and had grabbed his hand. Together they walked up to the house, the big dark man and the little blonde girl.

Livia opened the door, forcing her face into a smile.

It wasn't that difficult. Just looking at Tammy made her smile. She looked so happy, so full of life and excitement with her bright eyes and that springy step. She wore a short denim skirt and a flowered shirt and she looked lovely. Had Aurora taken her to shop for clothes? She pushed the thought away.

'Good morning, Clint, Tammy. Come on in. I have coffee in the kitchen.' She was proud of herself for sounding so normal. At least she thought she sounded normal.

They returned her greeting and moved inside. She closed the door against the oppressive heat. Inside the house was cool.

'It all looks so shiny and new!' exclaimed Tammy as they moved passed the living-room into the kitchen. 'But what about furniture, Daddy? Will Aunt Aurora come back and help us?'

'No, she'll be busy. We're on our own this time.'

'But she'll come and see us, won't she? She said she wanted to see the house, maybe at Christmas.'

Clint nodded. 'We can invite her for Christmas.'

Livia avoided Clint's face. She could not bear looking at him. She felt as if she were going to scream if she heard the name Aurora one more time. She turned her back and reached for the coffee-pot, then thought better of it. It might slip out of her hands.

She looked at Tammy. 'How about some apple juice? Or would you rather have orange?' Her voice sounded unsteady; she could hear it herself.

'I like everything,' Tammy stated. She grinned. 'I'll have apple juice, please.'

Livia poured and Tammy and Clint seated themselves at the kitchen table. Livia put the glass in front of Tammy and met Clint's eyes. 'Coffee?'

'Please.' He looked at her searchingly. 'You look tired,' he stated.

'I put in long hours. I wanted to get it finished before school started. I thought it would be better for Tammy.' It was part of the truth, if not the whole truth.

'Yes. That was considerate of you.'

She poured coffee in two mugs and sat down at the table, sliding one cup over towards Clint. 'Of course, you know you're not obliged to buy the house.'

'I know that.'

She nodded, looking not at his face, but at his big brown hand curving around the cup. Everything inside her ached. Every cell seemed aware of his presence. Her stomach churned and she couldn't drink her coffee. Tammy had finished her juice and slid off her chair.

'May I look around, Daddy?' she asked eagerly.

'We can all look around,' he said, and rose to his feet, picking up his coffee-cup to carry with him.

They made the rounds and inspected the lower floor rooms.

'It's so big!' Tammy cried. 'I can dance in here!' And she did, twirling and jumping around the empty rooms. Then she stopped in front of Clint.

'Where's my bedroom, Daddy? Can...may I see it?'

Clint smiled and ruffled her hair. 'Upstairs. Take your pick from the three to the left of the stairs.'

She rushed up the stairs and Livia watched her go, her heart pounding, waiting. It took less than a minute.

'Daddy! Daddy, come and look!' Tammy's excited voice filled the house.

Clint's brows lifted in surprise as he moved to the stairs. 'What?' he asked.

'Come and look!' said Tammy again.

Livia followed Clint up the stairs. Tammy rushed ahead of them into the decorated bedroom.

'Oh, Daddy, this is the most beautiful room I've ever seen!' Her face glowed, her eyes shone with such pure joy that Livia felt tears come to her eyes.

Clint's face registered surprise, then he smiled. 'It's beautiful.' He glanced at Livia, a question in his eyes.

Tammy took the doll off the bed. 'And look, Daddy, the doll's dress! It has daisies on it, just like the bedspread and the curtains!'

He stared at the dress. 'Yes,' he said then. 'You're right. This dress was yours, when you were little.'

Tammy's eyes grew even wider. 'Really?'

'Your great-grandma made it for you when you were a baby,' he said gently. 'She made the daisies herself.'

Her throat closed and Livia turned and fled back down the stairs, out of the kitchen door into the hot, humid morning. She gulped in air, her body rigid, her throat aching in the effort not to cry.

She was not going to break down and cry.

Footsteps came down the path. 'Livia?'

He sat down beside her on the old wooden bench. 'Something wrong?'

She shook her head, willing to be calm. 'I thought the two of you could look at the house by yourselves.'

'You did a magnificent job. Thank you.'

'It's my job,' she said evenly.

'You did more than your job, Livia. You put your soul into this house,' he said gently.

She didn't know what to say. She stared at her hands clasped in her lap.

'And the room you did for Tammy—that was above and beyond the call of duty.'

She gave a half-smile. 'I wanted to do it. It was fun. I only hoped you wouldn't mind.'

'No,' he said, and his voice sounded unsteady. 'You did it with love; how could I mind? And Tammy is so delighted.'

She looked away from him at the blooming crape myrtle a short distance away. 'It's so easy to make her happy. Everything seems so new and magical to her.'

'Yes,' he said soflty. 'Magic.' He reached out and took her hand, and his warm touch snapped her attention back to his face. His eyes met hers. 'I hurt you very badly, I know,' he said softly.

She slipped her hand out of his. She was afraid she'd shatter in a thousand pieces. 'Please don't do this to me. It's over. Let's just forget it.' She stood up from the bench. 'We should go inside and sign the contract and then make an appointment for the closing.' She wanted to get it all over with. Be done with it.

He came to his feet as well. 'It isn't over, Livia, you know that.'

She steeled herself. 'As soon as we've had the closing, it will be over,' she said tightly.

'There is a condition for my buying the house,' he said. 'I want a package deal.'

She raised her brows. 'What kind of package deal?'

'I'll buy the house if you come with it.'

Her heart stood still. 'If I come with it?' she repeated.

'This house won't be a real home without you, Livia.'

She closed her eyes and swallowed. 'I can't just stay here, Clint. It was a mistake for you to stay here in the beginning, and it will be a mistake for me to stay here with you now. I can't do it.'

'Remember once I said I didn't know how to live for the future?'

'Yes.' She remembered very well. She remembered everything he'd said.

'That's why I couldn't make any commitments. I'd made commitments once, and my life turned to ashes. The woman I loved died. The child I loved was taken away from me. I wasn't going to allow this to happen to me again.' He paused. 'Then fate threw me a curve.'

'Tammy,' she said.

'Yes.' His mouth quirked. 'Suddenly I had no choice. I had to make a commitment. I had to live for the future.'

She looked into his eyes. 'You did have a choice. You didn't have to take her. She isn't yours.'

He smiled a wry smile. 'Oh, she's mine all right, Livia. Not biologically, no, but she's mine in every possible way that counts.'

It was true. They belonged together. It was easy to see the way he looked at her, the love and pride in his eyes. The way Tammy looked at him, glowing, trusting, happy.

'And then there was you,' he went on. 'I was afraid to let you into my life and somehow get hurt again. I'd pushed you away, kept you at a distance, and refused to admit to myself how much I needed to love you, how much I needed for you to love me.' He paused. 'Aurora was coming to the States to do some postgraduate work at Harvard in the fall. When she offered to come early and help me, I took the opportunity with both hands. It was a way not to involve you any further, a way to stay away from you. I had to stay away from you to save me from myself. At least that's how I thought of it at the time.'

'And now?' The words came out on a whisper.

He gave a wry grin. 'I stopped deluding myself after Aurora called me a coward.'

She gaped at him. 'Aurora called you a *coward*?'

He smiled crookedly. 'She's a very smart woman. First time she set eyes on you, she knew the score. She said Gwen would be furious with me for letting happiness pass me by.'

'Gwen . . . your wife?'

He nodded. 'Gwen and Aurora were best friends since college.'

'Daddy! Livia! Where are you?' Tammy's voice sang out from the back porch.

'Over here!' Clint called and Tammy came running down the path.

'I'm going to swing,' she announced, and hopped on to the wooden swing hanging from the old gnarled apple tree. Several months ago, ages ago, Jack had replaced the old weathered ropes to keep his own little girls safe when they came to visit.

'I used to swing on that thing when I was a kid,' said Clint, watching Tammy with a smile.

'Look how high I can go, Daddy!' she shouted.

'Be careful!' he called out, then he glanced back at Livia.

'I have a future to live for,' he said quietly, 'sitting right there on the swing. Will you marry me and be part of it?'

For a moment she felt as if she were floating, as if the words had come to her in a dream. She felt his arms around her, his mouth by her ear. 'I love you, Livia. Forgive me for being such a fool.'

She felt a choking sensation, tears hot behind her eyes. 'I love you too,' she said huskily. 'Please, tell me this is not a dream. Say it again.'

'I love you. Will you marry me?' he said promptly.

She pressed herself closer into him, joy and love suffusing her. 'Yes,' she said huskily. 'Oh, yes, I'll marry you.' She kissed him drunkenly, then smiled through her tears. 'Just remember, you can never get away from me once we're married. I'd follow you to the ends of the earth.'

'You've proved that,' he said and gave her a long, heart-thrilling kiss. Then he raised his head and smiled into her eyes. 'I couldn't believe my eyes when I saw you sitting there in front of Pak Ubang's room. And then you trekked back with me, never complaining once.' He stroked her hair. 'You are one tough woman, Livia. You've got courage and compassion, and I've been crazy not to realise what I was trying to throw away.'

'And I should thank Aurora for pointing it out to you.' She gave a half-smile. 'I was jealous of her.'

'Jealous? Of what?'

'I thought you had some . . . arrangement with her.'

'What kind of arrangement?'

She groaned in embarrassment. 'You seemed to like each other so much, and . . .'

'We do. She was Gwen's best friend. What were you thinking?'

'I thought you might have some no-strings-attached arrangement with her, for whenever you were in Hong Kong. You kept clothes in her house.'

He tightened his arms around her and laughed out loud. 'You've got quite an imagination. There's nothing sexual between us; there never has been. She'd drive me up the wall within a day. She detests anything that creeps and crawls. She goes berserk over a fly in the kitchen.'

'Not your type,' Livia commented, feeling laughter bubble up inside her.

'No, but as a friend there's no better.' His hands slipped under her hair and cradled her head. He looked deep into her eyes—a smouldering look with a teasing glint of laughter. 'You, however, are very much my type,' he said softly, the sound of his voice like a caress. His mouth came down on hers again and all the worry and anguish of the last months melted away in the loving passion of his kiss.

It was the sound of smothered giggles that made them break apart.

Tammy was standing in front of them, her eyes huge with merriment, her hand covering her mouth, trying to suppress her laughter. Her hand dropped away.

'Oh, Daddy!' she said, collapsing into giggles. 'You were *kissing* her!'

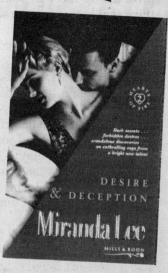
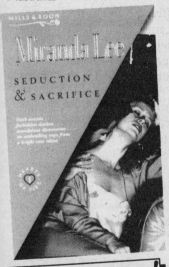

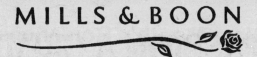

MILLS & BOON

Forthcoming Titles

DUET
Available in April

The Betty Neels Duet   **A SUITABLE MATCH**
THE MOST MARVELLOUS SUMMER

The Emma Darcy Duet   **PATTERN OF DECEIT**
BRIDE OF DIAMONDS

FAVOURITES
Available in April

NOT WITHOUT LOVE Roberta Leigh
NIGHT OF ERROR Kay Thorpe

LOVE ON CALL
Available in April

VET IN A QUANDARY Mary Bowring
NO SHADOW OF DOUBT Abigail Gordon
PRIORITY CARE Mary Hawkins
TO LOVE AGAIN Laura MacDonald

Next Month's Romances

Each month you can choose from a wide variety of romance with Mills & Boon. Below are the new titles to look out for next month, why not ask either Mills & Boon Reader Service or your Newsagent to reserve you a copy of the titles you want to buy — just tick the titles you would like and either post to Reader Service or take it to any Newsagent and ask them to order your books.

Please save me the following titles: Please tick   ✓

AN UNSUITABLE WIFE	Lindsay Armstrong	
A VENGEFUL PASSION	Lynne Graham	
FRENCH LEAVE	Penny Jordan	
PASSIONATE SCANDAL	Michelle Reid	
LOVE'S PRISONER	Elizabeth Oldfield	
NO PROMISE OF LOVE	Lilian Peake	
DARK MIRROR	Daphne Clair	
ONE MAN, ONE LOVE	Natalie Fox	
LOVE'S LABYRINTH	Jessica Hart	
STRAW ON THE WIND	Elizabeth Power	
THE WINTER KING	Amanda Carpenter	
ADAM'S ANGEL	Lee Wilkinson	
RAINBOW ROUND THE MOON	Stephanie Wyatt	
DEAR ENEMY	Alison York	
LORD OF THE GLEN	Frances Lloyd	
OLD SCHOOL TIES	Leigh Michaels	

If you would like to order these books in addition to your regular subscription from Mills & Boon Reader Service please send £1.90 per title to: Mills & Boon Reader Service, Freepost, P.O. Box 236, Croydon, Surrey, CR9 9EL, quote your Subscriber No:................................... (If applicable) and complete the name and address details below. Alternatively, these books are available from many local Newsagents including W H Smith, J Menzies, Martins and other paperback stockists from 8 April 1994.

Name:..
Address:..
....Post Code:..........................
To Retailer: If you would like to stock M&B books please contact your regular book/magazine wholesaler for details.

You may be mailed with offers from other reputable companies as a result of this application.
If you would rather not take advantage of these opportunities please tick box   ☐